TALES WITH A TWIST

by

C. K. Deatherage
Larry D. Rudder
B. David Spicer

RudderHaven
3014 Washington Ave
Granite City, IL 62040

Published by:

RudderHaven
3014 Washington Ave
Granite City, IL 62040
USA

First Softcover Printing, July 2014, RudderHaven
(ISBN 978-1-932060-12-6)

Cover Art: Eilee Fahnestock
Cover Design: Douglas Rudder
Illustrations: Eilee Fahnestock and Jeanette Deatherage

Printed in the United States of America

ISBN 978-1-932060-12-6

Table of Contents

When Duty Calls

The Shadow of the Truth
By C. K. Deatherage

I was named "Marvin" after my first-generation immigrant great-grandfather, Marvin Polaski. That alone keeps me from ever becoming popular at high school. I've been called Marvy, Marvin the Martian, Marble-brain, and other weird assortment of words that start with "Mar-." I have one teacher that routinely calls me "Martin." If I were six-foot-two and a lean, muscular basketball captain leading my team to the championship, perhaps then I could overcome the stigma of my out-dated name. But I'm a short, skinny five-five and a computer geek, so I strike out there too. It could have been worse. I could have inherited my great-grandfather's name on my mother's side—"Maurice."

Normally, I don't mind not being part of the "in" crowd. All my friends are fellow geeks, mostly gamers, like myself. But there's this one girl, Jessica Longford, in Chem Lab, that I totally crush on. Or did anyway before the day of my greatest humiliation.

Several of my classmates in Chemistry lab urged me to ask Jessica out on a date. "She's crazy about you," they said. So, after gathering all of my Junior-level courage, I dared to ask Jessica, a Senior, if she'd like to go out with me. She turned me down flat—and loudly—declaring she'd rather go out with a warthog than with a geek like me. The whole class heard and burst into laughter. The guys had set me up, and I had stupidly fallen for it. I hurriedly gathered up my books and left, ears burning red with embarrassment.

That night is when IT happened. As I lay in bed playing through the day's event like a B-rated horror flick, I gazed up at the solar mobile dangling from my ceiling and said, "I wish I could know when people are lying. And—I wish I could do something about it!" I wished many ugly things on the guys in Chemistry too, but didn't say any of those thoughts out loud. The next morning is when the gift, the talent, the power—whatever you want to call it—manifested itself. And it began with my brother Sheldon.

It was Saturday, and Dad stormed into the kitchen wearing his old holey sweats. It was a sure sign he meant to spend his weekend working in the garage. "Which one of you used my hammer and neglected to put it back?" he growled, eyeing us each with fatherly frustration.

Sheldon immediately popped back with, "Not me" and looked at Dad innocently with his large brown eyes. I, in turn, immediately knew he was lying. I don't know how I knew—I just did. But how could I prove it? Dad looked at me and said, "Well, Marvin?" I licked my lips and fumed. I would get the blame, of course. I always did. Sheldon could slide by on a lie more easily than a politician running for office. I think it was his puppy-dog eyes with their long eye-lashes. Mine were plain slate

2

blue. "I didn't use it—" I began, but Dad cut me off.

"One of you used my hammer, and I want to know where it is." His voice reverberated off the refrigerator and he stared directly at me. I, in turn, fastened my gaze on Sheldon who was calmly eating his cereal as if there were no father-volcano nearby ready to explode. In desperation, I folded my arms and thought, *Tell the truth, Sheldon.*

My brother stopped eating, put his spoon down, looked straight at Dad, and said, "I used your hammer yesterday, but the handle broke, so I hid it under the rags in the corner near the table saw." I blinked. Dad blinked. Sheldon blinked. I felt my jaw hanging open and snapped it shut. It was so unlike Sheldon to just blurt out the truth, especially when it might get him in trouble.

"Well," Dad said, calming down, "why didn't you say so to begin with? Why did you hide the hammer and why did you lie about it?"

Sheldon blinked again but continued. "I was afraid you'd be mad and I'd get punished, so I hid the broken hammer and lied about using it."

I felt my jaw begin to sag again. What had come over Sheldon? Dad must have been flummoxed as well. He hemmed and hawed a few moments then said, "Well, Sheldon, I probably would have been a bit put out since you used it without asking, but if you had told me the hammer had broken to begin with, I wouldn't have had to punish you as I must now do. You're grounded for the weekend for trying to wiggle out of your responsibility by hiding the hammer and lying about it."

Sheldon sighed. "Yes, sir." He twirled his spoon in his mushy cereal.

"But," Dad continued, "I'm glad you faced up to the truth and confessed what you did."

"I'm not," Sheldon said truthfully.

This set Dad back, but he recovered quickly. "Well, you should be. Telling the truth and owning up to things is a sign of maturity. Now, if you'll excuse me, I need to run to the hardware store to get a new hammer."

As Dad left, I started to ask Sheldon why he confessed but thought better of it, instead hurriedly spooning cereal into my mouth and making a fast getaway. I had to talk to Jeff, my best friend, and tell him about the weird events at breakfast—and ask how much damage control I needed to do with yesterday's disaster at school.

Jeff and I had been best friends since third grade when we had worn T-shirts to school sporting our favorite gaming characters. We discovered we liked to play the same games and frequently met online to battle villains or build worlds. As our tastes and skills matured, Jeff and I decided to form a business partnership designing computer games. We were working on a game that would blend the best of world-building, RPG, and combat into a spectacular MMORG experience. So far, we'd managed to crash both of our computers five times, mine barely recovering from "the blue screen of death" twice. Still we were determined to make this happen. In fact, we had planned to do some research today on some problematic programming issues, so as we walked to the library, I recounted the strange morning with Sheldon and started to describe my Friday fiasco at school.

"Yeah, I heard about Jessica," Jeff interrupted.

I groaned. "Probably the whole school's heard about it! How can I show my stupid face there on Monday?"

4

"You could get Bill and Tyler and the rest to confess to setting you up—just like you did with Sheldon," he offered, brushing a lock of shaggy blonde hair out of his eyes.

I snorted. "What do you mean? Sheldon just up and blurted out everything. I didn't do anything to him."

"Yeah you did. You knew he lied and then you *thought* at him. You told him to tell the truth in your mind—at least, that's what you told me."

"Well, yeah, but that was just coincidence—wasn't it?" I began to wonder for the first time if my wish last night had come true.

"Well, test it out on me. Ask me something. Then when I answer, you can tell me if I lied or told the truth."

"Okaaay," I said, unsure about the experiment. "Do you like Jessica Longford?"

"Absolutely not!" Jeff scowled.

He lied. I knew it. I swallowed. It was really awkward having my best friend like the same girl I crushed on. So I thought, *Tell the truth, Jeff.*

Jeff looked away a moment, cleared his throat then said, "Actually, I think Jessica is a real babe. If you didn't like her so much, and if I were more of a jock instead of a geek like you, I'd ask her out myself."

I just stood there for moment—we both did—feeling embarrassed. Finally, Jeff said, "Wow! Did you do that?"

I shrugged. "I dunno. Maybe. Sorry. It's just too . . . ."

"Weird?" he suggested.

"Yeah."

"Weirdly awesome! You *gotta* try this on the guys in Chem Lab Monday—they'll totally freak out! Man, I wish I could be there!"

5

Jeff had taken Photography instead of Chemistry that semester. I thought it was because he wanted to be near Tammi Winsted. Now I wasn't so sure. A new thought began to niggle at the back of my mind. "Hey, Jeff," I said, "I don't think it's a good idea for people to know that I can—you know—tell if they're lying or make them confess it."

Jeff nodded soberly, his blonde hair falling back into his eyes. "Yeah, I see what you mean. If people knew, they'd probably summon the men in black to haul you off to do experiments on you or turn you into some sort of governmental weapon."

"Ah—yeah, so we need to keep this hush-hush, okay?" I actually hadn't thought of being carted off by government thugs to be turned into a lab rat. I just worried that I would change from a *geek* to a *freak* at school. But Jeff had a point.

"How do you do it?" he asked.

"Do what?"

"You know, the mind-reading thing."

I shrugged. "I really don't know. It just started all of a sudden." I didn't want to tell him about last night's wish. It sounded too surreal.

Jeff pressed on. "What's it like?

"Well . . ." I paused, trying to wrap my thoughts around the feeling, "It's like knowing the *shadow* of the truth. I can't really tell when people are telling the *truth*—only when they aren't. It's like seeing the shadow but not the light that cast it."

Jeff was getting more excited. "It's like you've got these cool superpowers. Think of all the good you could

6

do—forcing the news media to stick to the facts, exposing false politicians— "

I interrupted. "Anybody with half a brain already knows most politicians lie to get elected."

"Yeah, but there are all sorts of people with half a brain that believe them." Jeff grinned, then slapped his leg excitedly. "Hey! You could be a lawyer! Think how you could tell who was lying and make them reveal the truth on the stand!" He deepened his voice. "A lawyer by day—the *Confessor* by night!"

I laughed. "I can't be a confessor—I'm Baptist!"

"No, no, I mean that's your hero name—The Confessor!"

I shook my head. Jeff was really into superheroes—he'd seen all the latest movies that had come out over the years. He had even scavenged the cardboard display models from the store advertizing the latest superhero movie and plastered them all over his room. Of course, I couldn't criticize him—I was part of the outdated Pokemon club at school and had every book, movie, and game card on the topic. Another reason I was a geek. But maybe Jeff had point. What was it that Spider-man's uncle said? *With great power comes great responsibility.* Maybe I was supposed to do something great, something that would benefit my fellow man—or woman—with my *gift*.

"I'll think about my future career later. Let's just see what happens on Monday," I said.

Monday happened just as Jeff had predicted. The guys in class started to tease me about Jessica, and I confronted them with their lie. "You told me Jessica crushed on me," I accused when the teacher was out of the room.

"Eeew!" Jessica said, glaring angrily at everyone.

"No we didn't!" Tyler blurted. I tried hard not to grin as I thought, *Tell the truth, Tyler.*

"Actually," Tyler continued, "we thought it would be totally hilarious to watch you make a fool of yourself with Jessica, so we told you she really liked you. But of course, she doesn't—like you, I mean."

"Tyler!" Bill stormed.

I thought, *Tell the truth, Bill.*

"Tyler, you stupid!—yeah, all right, so we did set you up, Marvin. But you fell for it, and well . . ." Bill floundered as if realizing what he was saying.

"You guys!" Jessica stormed. "You're just awful!" Then she looked at me with those beautiful green eyes and gave a half smile. "Sorry, Marvin. I shouldn't have said what I did about you. You're pretty nice—just not my type. Okay?"

I smiled and nodded. I was still spurned, but in a polite way. Best of all, she didn't lie.

Later, at lunch Jeff plopped down next to me in the cafeteria and pumped air with his fist.

"Whew! I heard what happened in Chem Lab. Man, you've got the power, Marvin!"

"Sshh," I said, glancing around.

"Yeah, right," Jeff whispered, twisting some spaghetti onto his fork. He winked and mouthed, "The Confessor!" Then around a mouthful of noodles, he added, "Tomorrow's Career Day. They're going to have over 50 career booths. I heard there are five booths representing various computer fields. Wanna scope them out tomorrow?"

"I'm still thinking," I said.

"Yeah, but I bet I know what's top on your list!" he grinned. I sighed. He wasn't lying.

I came home from Career Day with only one large packet to show for my research.

"A lawyer?" Dad said when he saw it. "You want to be a lawyer? I'm impressed. When did you decide on this?"

"Recently," I answered.

"It'll take a lot of work, but your grades are up there. If this is what you really want, your Mom and I will support you all the way."

"Thanks, Dad." I must not have sounded very convincing because Dad paused and eyed me firmly. "Why a lawyer, Marvin? Last I knew you wanted to go into Computer Programming."

I swallowed, squared my shoulders and said, "Well, I think I've got a gift for it. And gifts should be used responsibly, don't you think?"

Dad nodded.

"So, I want to be a lawyer," I declared.

It was the shadow of the truth.

Field Call
by C. K. Deatherage

I sigh and run my finger as far as I can reach beneath the Suppressor collar that encircles my neck. It must be hot today because even this far below ground, the metal of the collar makes me sweat. I lean back against the gray cement-block wall of my cell, knees drawn up to my chest, while I pick at the rips in the Army-green wool blanket on my cot. I glance at the faint white slash marks I make each morning on the wall, using the edge of my dulled spoon, before they take away my tray and its utensils. It's been six months and seventeen days since my captivity. I wonder what's been happening in the Resistance against Ruler-Commander Sarx—or if there remains a Resistance at all.

I close my eyes and let my mind wander to the days before Sarx and his attempt at world-wide domination. My sister and I had joined the League of Guardians two years ago. The Guardians, as they are typically called, consist of people endowed with mutant abilities and/or intelligence. After the fall-out from Supernova 314 hit Earth, genetic mutations began occurring in the succeeding generations, resulting in the formation of—for lack of a better word—superhumans. I possess the ability to draw on energy around me and channel it into various types of force-fields or energy surges. As I draw in the surrounding energy, a fluctuating glow permeates my body. So I was assigned the code-name "Glimmer" by the Guardians, but I prefer to go by my given name of Nooma.

My younger sister lacks the spectacular abilities that many superhumans possess, but she developed a high-level intelligence with a photographic memory. The Guardians assigned her to computer technology: she can design, decipher, hack into, and memorize anything that uses computer programming. No rogue nation or terrorist group was safe from her probes. Naturally, the Guardians gave her the code-name "Hacker." Like her big sister, she prefers to go by her given name of Whilla—Whil for short.

The Guardians are essential for maintaining peace in a world that produces superhumans—not all of whom choose to use their powers for the good of humankind. And Whil and I were honored to have been accepted into the Academy and, later, into the League itself. We worked well together—I on the outside, protecting, defending; Whil on the inside, spying, designing. We were a unit—essential, it turns out, to the Guardian-led resistance against Ruler-Commander Sarx.

Sarx was not satisfied to use his super-abilities for the good of humanity—he wanted to dominate humankind. Nation after nation fell to his superior strategy, weaponry, and mutant army, until only small pockets of resistance remained scattered across the continents. The Guardians linked these resistance movements together and searched for a way to defeat Sarx. Whil and I were part of the Resistance: she helping to coordinate our attacks, I helping to carry them out. We were a team—until six months and seventeen days ago when she betrayed my unit to Ruler-Commander Sarx.

We fought against indescribable odds. Many were killed. A few were taken prisoners and Suppressor collars electronically locked around our necks to neutralize our mutant powers. We were blindfolded and taken to different holding areas. I think I'm at Sarx's headquarters in Brazil, based on the snatches of conversation I hear in the corridors and the fact that Sarx would keep me near to make sure my sister, his new computer-savvy recruit, would stay in line. With her knowledge of Guardian infrastructure, Sarx would deem her invaluable in crushing the Resistance.

I rub at my collar again, then freeze as I hear footsteps outside my door. The electronic lock clicks and blinks off, the door opening inward. Two gray-clad guards step in, laser rifles held ready. Then Ruler-Commander Sarx himself enters, his well-cut uniform a darker gray than his underlings, his salt-and-pepper hair cut military short, a black pencil-thin moustache resting on his upper lip. His eyes are as gray as the walls and uniforms surrounding me, but they snap with fire. He clicks his black-booted heels together and bows slightly. "Your presence, my dear Glimmer, is requested in the Command Center."

I don't move. "Who requests it? You? I think I'd rather stay here and play with the beetles." A black one is crawling at the base of the wall even as I speak.

The Ruler-Commander's smile is edged with malice. "I do not make requests, Glimmer. I command. It is your sister who insists on your presence. I think she wishes to watch your reaction as we commence our final countdown to Operation Elimination, which will remove all vestiges of your annoying Resistance. She has proven to be invaluable to me, and I find her request most interesting. I, too, would enjoy watching your reaction. We think alike, your sister and I."

"I didn't know Whil had suffered dementia," I say, arms crossed, still leaning back against the wall.

Sarx drops his smile. He signals to his guards. "Bring her!" he says, turning on one heel and striding from the room.

I try not to wince as the guards grab either arm and roughly haul me to my feet. They march me between them down the corridor, their booted feet making a sharp clack on the concrete next to the slap of my cold bare ones. We reach an elevator with red doors. I watch as we ascend to subfloor 11, which is still underground as is the entire base, making it a difficult target for the Resistance. My prison cell is on subfloor 33. I'm curious which floor houses the Cloning Chamber—one of the main reasons for Sarx's success.

There have been several assassination attempts against Sarx—completed ones, in fact. But the Ruler-Commander uses the "live-cell" cloning technique—more successful than clones derived from hair or dead skin cells—which, coupled with cranial implants that update his clones with his memories even while they remain in suspended animation, makes him almost impossible to eliminate. Each time the Resistance has managed to execute Sarx, a new Sarx emerges from suspension, complete with the original's thoughts, memories, and plans. I don't know how many cloned generations the current Sarx is, but it doesn't matter. Trying to kill the Ruler-Commander is like trying to kill the fabled Hydra. Lop off one head and two more grow back. Unless we can locate all of his bases with their hidden Cloning Chambers, the world will never be rid of the Ruler-Commander.

The elevator stops, as do my ruminations about Sarx, and the doors slide open directly into the Command Center. Multiple screens run two-thirds of the way around the room. Lights from rows of consoles blink off-and-on, looking like warped Christmas decorations. The room is bustling with activity—techs roaming from one section to another, murmuring to their comrades. But center front is what grabs my attention.

My sister stands up from where she had been seated at a large console. Beside her is the Ruler-Commander. Both turn to gaze at me. I swallow. Her eyes seem hard. She's dressed in a form-fitting dark gray jacket-trouser set, similar to that of Sarx, her auburn hair pulled back in a tight bun. I notice multiple colored bars on the breast of her uniform. She's progressed rapidly in the months we've been here. I wonder how many of the Resistance died to further her rank.

"Hello, Bigster," she says. I can't help but wince at the term. When she was a toddler, "big sister" came out "bigster." It became her nickname for me and has stuck ever since. It stings now, to hear it used under these circumstances. The Ruler-Commander notices my discomfiture and smiles.

"Welcome to the Command Center, Glimmer." He waves at the video panels on the curved wall. "In a few moments, you will witness the utter elimination of the Resistance and the League of Guardians. Then the world can finally settle down under my rule."

I know what he means. With multiple clones waiting in suspended animation, Sarx could rule indefinitely. I shift, the cold from the concrete floor radiating up through my bare feet to send a shiver through the rest of my body. Sarx sees this and his smile broadens. "We have placed strategically located satellites in Earth's orbit armed with specially designed lasers. Lasers which are pointed at all bases of operation belonging to the Resistance and the League of Guardians—thanks to your sister."

I say nothing and try to remain stony-faced.

The Ruler-Commander turns toward the video panels. "Commence Operation Elimination," he says boldly. Whil is still gazing at me. Then she nods, looks down at the control panel next to her and pushes a single brightly lit button.

Instant pandemonium.

Warning sirens blast through the air. Lights flash. Techs dash from one console to the next. The images flicker on the video panels and go black. Then I feel a soft buzz at my neck as the Suppressor collar disengages. Immediately, I feel the surge of high-level energy as I begin to absorb its potency. It's my turn to smile as the "glimmer" begins to pass over my hands and body. I hope in the current panic that no one will notice until I have charged up.

"What's happening?" Sarx demands, grabbing Whil by her right arm.

She shakes her head. "We've been hacked."

"The Guardians?" he hisses.

"Looks that way." Her hands roam over the control panel, pushing various sequences of buttons and sliding levers.

"Override them! We need to regain control!"

Before Whil can respond, a tech calls a warning. "Ruler-Commander!" He points at me, and Sarx's eyes follow the direction to my glowing body. He curses and tries to draw the laser pistol strapped to his right leg. I laugh and thrust my arms out, hands pointed up, as I envelop the room in an immobilizing force-shield. The sirens ring and the lights continue to flash, but all movement ceases. All except for the two people standing in front of me. Sarx manages to pull his pistol free and fires at me. The laser is absorbed into my force shield and adds to the energy output flowing from my body. I smile.

"Drop it, Sarx."

Sarx whirls to face Whil. She's pointing her own laser pistol at him. It's a different design from any I've seen before. Sarx notices the design as well. He pales and slowly lowers his pistol, crouching and placing it on the floor. Then he stands, raising both hands in apparent surrender.

"You're a plant," he says quietly and shakes his head. "A very good one." He looks at me. "She betrayed hundreds of your comrades and gave away countless League secrets in order to gain my trust."

Perhaps he is hoping to turn me against my sister, start some sort of in-fighting to his advantage. It doesn't work. I merely nod soberly and say, "We know. It was a calculated risk we were all willing to take—and it's paid off."

He shakes his head. "You can't stop me that easily."

"We have." Whil's voice is steady. "At this very moment, the satellite lasers are configured to destroy each of your bases, including all Cloning Chambers." She glances at a screen on her console and smiles. "You now have no bases, no standing army, and no clones." Again, she glances at the console screen. She nods. "Your satellites with their lasers have just self-destructed."

Sarx's face is contorted in a snarl as he steps toward her. I prepare to expand my immobilizing shield to capture him, but Whil intervenes. She raises her laser pistol and tightens her finger on its trigger. "Just give me an excuse, Sarx. Any excuse will do. Move a pinky and you're current body is history. There are no more replacement clones."

Sarx stops, hands clenched at his side, pulse pounding in his temple. Slowly he relaxes and a faint smile plays on his lips. "I'll return, you know."

Whil smiles back. "Yes, I know. I know everything, Sarx. They don't call me the Hacker for nothing. Everything that was in your network is common knowledge to me—and that includes your neural connection to the clones. I know your thoughts, your plans, and your countermoves. I know that you have plants in the Resistance that will work to re-clone you before your execution. And that is why I can't let you live, even to stand trial."

Before either Sarx or I can react, a silent white flash engulfs my vision. I feel a strong surge of energy, then I blink and gaze at the spot where Sarx had stood. There is nothing but a white ashy-looking patch on the concrete floor. I switch my gaze to the laser pistol Whil holds. Several lights flash along its barrel. I blink and shake my head. "What is *that*?" I ask.

17

Whil draws a deep breath and begins keying a sequence into the flashing lights and buttons on the pistol. "It's a miniature version of the lasers Sarx had orbiting around the Earth, ready to take out anyone that stood in his way."

I exhale. "So, Sarx is gone."

Whil nods. "Every shred of usable DNA."

I shake my head, flexing my fingers as I continue to channel the surrounding energy into the immobilizing shield. "That wasn't the plan. He was supposed to stand trial for his crimes."

"And give his plants time and access to steal enough DNA to clone him again? Sorry, Nooma, but this is my Field Call."

I nod. The Guardians allow their operatives to make "Field Calls," a change of plan, based on circumstances beyond the scope or knowledge of higher officers. Of course, operatives have to give account for their call—and I have a feeling the higher-ups aren't going to be pleased with Whil's summary execution of the Ruler-Commander.

Whil sighs and waves a hand over the blinking console behind her. "The rest of the bases are destroyed. Since the base here is going to be captured by the Resistance in about . . ." She glances at the monitor on her console, "twelve minutes, I left this one standing. And I've erased all records and archives in the network. Only those programs essential to gaining access to the base are still running." Whil looks up at me, her eyes bright. "Basically, all traces of the Ruler-Commander and his plans for world conquest are gone. His network is wiped clean. His clones destroyed. His DNA non-existent."

I say nothing. I know the Guardians would have wanted access to that information for the trial—a trial that no longer has a criminal to try. Whil seems to guess my thoughts. "It was too dangerous, Nooma. His plans, his weapon designs, his strategies—leaving those intact would be just as bad as leaving his clones alive. It would mean another Ruler-Commander would someday emerge. Possibly from the ranks of the Guardians themselves. Remember, Sarx has plants in the Resistance."

I nod. "So, basically, all traces—living and digital—of the Ruler-Commander have been extinguished."

Whil is silent a moment. "Not quite. There's one repository of information left."

She punches a few more codes into the pistol she's holding. My heart begins to beat faster. "Whil, what are you doing?"

She takes another deep breath. The laser pistol she's holding begins to hum. "I wasn't exaggerating about knowing every detail of Sarx's plans and thoughts. You know my photographic memory. And . . . there are ways to extract that information, highly unpleasant ways. I can't let that happen."

"Whil . . ." I swallow. "Whil, don't!"

She hugs the humming pistol to her chest. "I love you, Bigster," she says. There's a brilliant but silent flash, another surge of energy in my force shield—and another white ashy circle on the floor.

"Whil," I whisper, slumping, almost losing control over my immobilizing shield. Tears blur my eyes as I struggle to breathe, to hold on until the Resistance arrives. I don't have long to wait. I hear the door swoosh open behind me and heavy steps enter. A lot of heavy steps.

"You can let dem go, Glimmer. We have dem covered."

It's Ghurka, a Nepalese Guardian whose mutant skills include high speed and precision blade-throwing, a deadly combination. We've worked together before. I lower my arms and let the energy drain from me. The unit takes care of the Ruler-Commander's techs and soldiers as I continue to gaze at the spot where my sister had stood. Ghurka comes up to stand beside me.

"The plan, it worked well," he says.

I nod.

"Where is Sarx?"

I gesture at the first white spot on the floor and say, "Field Call."

"Ah . . . Yours?"

I shake my head. "Whil's."

Ghurka is silent a moment, his dark eyes following mine to the ashy circles. Then softly he asks, "And Whil?"

I breathe deeply, sorrow and pride vying for command of my voice as I answer: "Field Call."

As the Bat Flies
by C. K. Deatherage

I listen, straining to hear what is being said in the next room. I can hear voices—three, in fact—but I can discern no words. I sigh and lean back in the foam padded chair. Its cushions enfold my body. The headrest fits snugly around my temples. I don't like that. It muffles my sense of hearing, and that is all-important to me. You see, I am blind. I've been that way from birth. Probably a defect in one or the other of my parents' genes left over from Influenza X. They were among the lucky one-third of the population who survived. It took fourteen months to finish burying the other two-thirds. Influenza X swept through the States like a maelstrom, swallowing whole families, whole towns, and nearly whole cities. That was 27 years ago, and our population is still struggling to recover.

I lean forward, resting my elbows on my knees. I lower my head so to others it will appear as if I am staring at the floor. Of course, I'm not. I can't stare at anything. But I've been told the vacant gaze of the blind can be disconcerting to the seeing, so I wear the traditional dark glasses and try to turn my head in the direction of

21

those speaking to me to make them feel more comfortable. However, they took my glasses when I entered the building, along with my wallet, my talking watch, my Braille cell phone, and my apartment keys. So now I turn my "gaze" to the floor in order not to make any one watching me feel uncomfortable. I don't want them to be uncomfortable. I want them to like me, to hire me to be a part of the Animal-Human Empath Project or AHEP. You can't imagine how much I want that.

After Influenza X finished its devastating course, the survivors began moving. Many came to the cities trying to find food, medicine, and other supplies that just weren't to be had in the country. Empty houses and apartments, even garages and storage sheds, became new homes to survivors. No one objected—there were too few left to object. Besides, the cities needed more manpower. But still it was not enough. Crime was rampant and there were not enough police or National Reserve units to handle the situation. That's when the Animal-Human Empath Project was implemented.

Animals had not been affected by the Influenza X virus, and a group of scientists, zoologists, doctors, and robotics experts began to put together a program whereby physically challenged humans—and there were a lot of us—could mentally link with a creature partner via an "empath chip," a tiny living computer, part machine, part virus, implanted in both brains. The animal would become the human partner's eyes, ears, feet, and—well—paws. Some acted as scouts, others as Enforcers, and still others as rescue units, bringing medicines and supplies in canisters or packs attached to their backs. Animals can scramble into places humans can't go. And, if needed, they have built-in defenses: teeth and claws. The project has been in place for four years now, and as I have completed the preliminary training, I am ready to be evaluated for the program.

The voices grow silent, and I continue leaning forward, relaxed, trying not to look as if I had been listening. I hear the swoosh of a nearby door, off to my right. Several scents catch my nose—aftershave and something I can't quite place—rather musty-smelling.

"Mr. Samuel Beckworth?"

I stand to my feet, keeping the edge of the chair against my legs for a reference point. I turn my head in the direction of the speaker and answer, "Yes, sir."

"Please be seated, Mr. Beckworth," the rather raspy voice continues. I slowly sink back into the cushioned chair, leaning forward slightly. My pulse picks up a few beats, wondering if the formality of the speaker is a good thing—or a bad sign.

"I want to congratulate you on finishing the prerequisite program with such high marks." The speaker pauses, and I wet my lips nervously. "I welcome you to the Animal-Human Empath Project, Mr. Beckworth, as our latest recruit. Now, I want you to meet your partner. Please sit back and relax as I place her on your lap."

I lean back obediently, keeping my head bent forward so the headrest will not cover my ears. A small, warm body is settled on my thighs. From this creature comes the musty scent I smelled earlier. *Well*, I think, *I didn't draw a tiger or even a large dog. Maybe a cat.*

"Go ahead, Mr. Beckworth, you may gently touch your partner. She's used to human handling."

Locating the creature by scent and her position on my lap, I slowly bring my right hand down to touch

23

her. Soft, furry, tiny pointed ears. I continue running my hand along her back. No tail, well, maybe a stub of one. Too small to be a cat. A hamster maybe? I hadn't known they'd employed animals that small. I feel a twinge of disappointment. Then my fingers find her wings, soft filmy leather, tiny claws at the ends. A bat!

I must have said the word out loud because the raspy voice gives a soft laugh. "Yes, Mr. Beckworth. A bat. A little brown bat or *Myotis lucifugus*, to be exact. A common species in North America. She is 'fixed' so as not to be distracted by mating urges, and before she begins her nightly tour, she will be fed, so that her natural instinct to hunt will not conflict with your mind control.

"Mind control?" For some reason I had thought of it as more of a partnership.

"Yes, Mr. Beckworth. We need scouts and police and rescue personnel—and no animal, no matter how smart or well-trained, can do these jobs adequately on their own. You, as the human factor, will be in control at all times."

"I see." I sit quietly, gently stroking my little brown bat, wishing I knew what brown looks like. My younger brother once described brown as the color of soil. So I've always thought of brown as moist and gritty. My "partner" is neither—except for her tiny cold nose. That is suitably moist.

I clear my voice. "Why a bat, sir?" I'm not sure if the raspy voice is Lt. Rimon or Sgt. Schmidt.

Another soft laugh. "Well, Mr. Beckworth, if I gave you, say, a Border Collie, you could use its hearing and sense of smell and the touch of its pad on the sidewalk, but how would you interpret the data flowing in from its eyes? You've never had vision, as I understand it, so the data would be mind-boggling. As it is, you will need to adjust to the way little Nedda 'sees'—for in her own way, she does see."

I nod. I had hoped to have a true seeing animal, just to experience what vision looks like, but I can understand the policy—even if it is a tremendous disappointment. I hear the speaker shift and feel his body heat as he leans forward and gently scoops up Nedda from my lap. His aftershave is spicy, like pepper mixed with mint. Then he stands up.

"Tomorrow," he says, "you and Nedda will have your implants. Then in three days' time you will begin your training."

"Why three days, Sir?" I ask.

"We need to make sure neither of you rejects your implant. It's been known to happen, though rarely."

Great, another delay. Another hurdle to worry about.

*   *   *   *

Three days have passed with no negative impact from the surgery other than a mild headache for several hours the first day. Nedda and I are in the Noob Room— at least, that's what the recruits call it. It's a large empty room with padded walls and one straight-backed metal chair in its center. It's empty so that animal and human will not have anything to bump into while learning to navigate together. Nedda is resting on my lap as I sit. They haven't activated our implants yet, but I try to breathe evenly, keeping my nervousness at bay so as not to affect Nedda while we wait. I assume the room is dark, or nearly so, since Nedda and I will be on night duty.

A voice speaks over the intercom. "All right, Mr. Beckworth. Try turning on your implant, please."

I swallow. No one had said *I* had to turn on the implant. I thought it was done remotely. Then again, I suppose I must be able to turn it on and off at will as I wouldn't want to be connected to Nedda 24/7. I breathe deeply and focus on the area of my shaved head where the implant had been inserted. Nothing. Nedda continues to sit placidly on my lap. If bats could purr, I think she'd be doing so. I, however, am beginning to sweat.

"Try thinking of Nedda, Mr. Beckworth. Try to get inside her mind. Think what she must be thinking. Sense what she is experiencing right now," the voice continues patiently.

I refocus my thoughts down toward the little brown bat in my lap. Instinctively, I begin to stroke her back with my right forefinger. Suddenly, I feel a strange though pleasant sensation travel from my neck to the small of my back. I freeze. The feeling vanishes. Then I try stroking Nedda again, thinking of her all the while. Again, I feel the sensation along my neck and back. I give a soft laugh and say, "I can feel my finger running down my own back as I pet her!"

"Good, very good, Mr. Beckworth. You are connected. Now try to smell what she smells," the voice says.

I obey. Immediately, my sinuses are assaulted by the scent of my deodorant—which seems sickeningly sweet—and the aroma of the antiseptic used to clean the room after the last occupants, which is so pungent, it almost brings tears to my eyes. I had noticed neither before connecting with Nedda.

"Now, Mr. Beckworth, listen to what Nedda hears."

I refocus. Suddenly, my hearing becomes hollow, sounds echoing off the walls through the empty space.

Beyond the walls, I can discern whispers, scratching, the moan of metal as the building shifts ever so slightly. I think I can faintly hear a dog bark.

"Try to see what Nedda sees, Mr. Beckworth." I flinch at the words, not out of fear but because they seem so loud.

Again I refocus and the sounds in my mind begin to coalesce into an image. It is a square, no, a cube with a funny man-shaped blob in the middle. Everything seems to be outlined in some sort of color—my guess is yellow or orange since it reminds me of the heat of fire, and my brother once described fire using those colors. The colored cube flickers as I hear Nedda giving off high-pitched squeaks. She's using echolocation, and the flickering outline is how the sound waves bounce back to her from her surroundings. I raise my left hand, and the man-blob raises its left hand. I wiggle my fingers and see the orange-yellow movement of the five digits. I almost weep. It's the first time I've ever seen my own hand.

"It's time to fly, Mr. Beckworth." The unseen instructor's voice seems almost soft. I wonder if I had let a tear or two slip past my eyelids. I take a deep breath and mentally tell Nedda to fly. I feel her hop twice on my lap while at the same time I feel the cloth of my trousers against the soles of my feet. It is strange, awkward, yet exhilarating to experience both my own senses and Nedda's at the same time. She stretches out her soft leathery wings and with one more hop, she's airborne. And I'm flying!

We circle the room, the walls glowing brighter the closer we approach them. We veer and dip and turn. Sometimes I direct the movements and sometimes Nedda. I see myself sitting in the glowing chair—a human outlined in yellow-orange. I've been told I have sandy-blond hair and green eyes, a sharp nose, and a strong chin with just a hint of a dimple. The nose, the chin, and the dimple I can touch, but the sandy-blond hair and green eyes are beyond my concept. Even now the only colors I can see, if I have those described right, are yellow and orange. Yellow for close objects, orange for farther away. Still, I am seeing—and in limited color—for the first time in my life—and flying! This time, I feel the tears on my cheeks. But I don't care.

The voice breaks in on our flight. "You've done extremely well, Mr. Beckworth. Tomorrow, you and Nedda will start training in the Obstacle Room. You may recall Nedda to your lap now."

Reluctantly, I summon Nedda back. She flaps and hops a couple of times on my lap, then nestles against my left arm while I stroke her with my right forefinger. "You did good, girl," I whisper.

"Please disengage the connection, Mr. Beckworth."

I'm reluctant to let go of my new senses—or my new little furry friend—but I obey. The room goes black, my hearing seems to fold in on itself. I almost panic, thinking I've gone deaf. Then I hear the door open and footsteps approach. Someone lifts Nedda from my lap. Someone else hands me my walking cane and assists me to the door.

"You did very well today, Mr. Beckworth, better than most recruits." The voice belongs to a woman, Dr. MacKenzie. "I think it will only be a few weeks before you join our active duty officers in patrolling the city streets."

"Thank you, Ma'am," I say, and my heart beats with pride and thankfulness towards a certain little brown bat.

*   *   *   *

It takes more like a month for Nedda and me to learn to navigate through the simulations in the Obstacle Room. It's my fault it takes so long. I have to learn what things like trash cans, dumpsters, mail boxes, light posts, and park benches look like. Humans are fairly easy to recognize. Animals take a little doing to figure out which kind they are. But at last I gain enough visual reference points that the higher-ups feel Nedda and I are ready to meet our partner empaths. Nedda is the scout, looking for problem areas, but a small bat can't do much to help in troubled spots. She alerts me to problems and I'm supposed to alert my co-worker and his or her animal empath to go to the site with the appropriate aid or law enforcement. I try not to be nervous as I hold Nedda in my lap, stroking her back, and waiting for my partner.

The room we are in, as outlined by Nedda's echo-location, is a small rectangle with two couches, a low table, what looks like a large potted plant, and a trash can. There are other rectangles lying on the table—probably magazines. I assume none are in Braille, so I don't bother picking one up.

With Nedda's enhanced hearing, I discern footsteps in the hallway approaching us. Two-footed steps and the sharp click of claws on linoleum of a four-footed animal. There is also another sound—a sort of sliding or rolling. The door opens and the travelers enter. I see a tall man pushing a chair. A wheel chair! It's difficult to see whether or not the person in the wheel chair is male or female—the image is less distinct as Nedda's attention is riveted on the other animal. A dog. A large dog. From the slope of its back, its long snout, and the pointed ears, I guess it could be a German Shepherd or some sort of Shepherd mix. We used to have a German Shepherd when I was a kid, and I had loved running my hands through her fur and feeling along her head and back. I'm comfortable with a Shepherd. Nedda feels me relax and her nervousness over the dog diminishes. She, too, relaxes against my left arm—her favorite spot—and begins surveying the other inhabitants in the room. I can see the person pushing the wheelchair is a tall male, while the occupant of the chair is a female with shoulder-length hair.

"Officer Samuel Beckworth, please meet your empath partners Officer Michelle Stevens and Hunter," the male says. I recognize the raspy voice as Lt. Rimon's. Rimon wheels Michelle closer so we can shake hands. With Nedda's heightened senses, I smell several scents on the woman—strawberry shampoo; a sweet, baby-powder deodorant; and the waxy aroma of make-up. I wonder what Officer Stevens scents from me through Hunter. I'm glad I had taken a shower this morning. Hunter has a strong odor of—well, *dog*—a little pungent, like freshly turned wet dirt.

"Hello, Officer Beckworth," Michelle says. Her voice is a mellow alto, firm and warm.

"Please, call me Sam," I say, shaking her hand.

"Then make it Michelle," she answers. I think she smiles, but the glow from Nedda's echolocation is not that precise. She turns toward Hunter and says, "Hunter, go see Sam."

The dog moves toward me, ears alert. I hold out my hand for him to sniff. Then I begin to scratch him between the ears. He's polite, but he keeps turning his head toward Nedda, who is shrinking back against my arm, not quite sure what to make of the huge beast standing before her. I try to send encouraging feelings toward Nedda.

Suddenly, Hunter leans forward and sniffs Nedda. Then, his long tongue thrusts out and gives her a lick. I'm not sure if he's viewing her as a potential snack or as a tiny buddy. Then his head lifts and he backs away and sits beside the wheelchair. Michelle must have given the order to back off. Nedda shuffles her wings and tries to shake off the dog saliva. I don't think she appreciated the morning bath.

"Sorry about that," Michelle says.

"No, that's good," Lt. Rimon interjects. "The animals need to know and feel comfortable around each other. You'll start working together in the Obstacle Room tomorrow." He turns towards me. "Officer Stevens and Hunter have been with us for three years. We always pair rookies with experienced empath partners."

"That's good," I say, and it is. Michelle and Hunter will know their way around our "beat" pretty well and be able to handle most situations. Nedda and I are in good hands.

The training goes well. At first, Michelle and I are in the Obstacle Room with our animals partners. Then we are moved to a different room, an "Observation Room," they call it. Not that we can observe directly, but we—at least I—must learn to control our animal partners from a distance. This requires me to connect more closely with Nedda and learn to subordinate my own senses to hers. I lose nearly all awareness of my immediate surroundings—even the padded chair I'm sitting in recedes from my consciousness—as I bond more closely with Nedda and where she is. After nine days, Lt. Rimon declares we are ready to begin our rounds.

We have the northwest corner of Central Park. Once the home of vagrants and joggers, the park has become a refugee camp as more and more people flock in from the surrounding countryside. Tents and storage sheds turned into living quarters dot the landscape along with a multitude of Porta-Potties and a few buildings that house showers and laundry facilities. The city does its best to relocate the refugees as quickly as possible, but it can still take months before people are granted permanent accommodations. Families are given priority—sometimes to the anger and frustration of singles and couples who have been there longer. And crime—especially theft and assault—is fairly high. The few police can't be everywhere at once—thus the need for the AHEP officers. Our team is one of seven that patrol the area.

Michelle and I, along with the other six teams, are stationed in the back of a large semi-trailer-turned-Command-Center just outside the park. I've only "seen" the inside of the trailer once when Nedda was with me. It was a confusing picture with chairs and consoles and computers and other equipment hard to identify. It was too bright for Nedda to distinguish things clearly, so my image of the Command Center is a little fuzzy. However, since all I do is sit in a padded chair with my eyes closed directing Nedda, I'm not really concerned with my surroundings.

The first three months go by in standard routine: locate trouble areas, notify Michelle, who sends Hunter to break up fights or scare off potential thieves. If Hunter's presence isn't enough to stop the crime, then human police are called in. The animals are pretty safe—they wear special yellow vests with the AHEP emblem stamped on it. (Nedda has a small yellow vest herself, though her tiny size makes it hard to see the markings.) It's a crime to harm an animal empath—with a high penalty. To kill one is treated the same as human murder. Most criminals just break and run when we come on the scene—or at least when Hunter does. Nedda is not much of a threat, and she usually flies high enough the criminals don't even know she's there. But the large German Shepherd with his long white incisors and warning growl is another matter.

Then a subtle shift begins to occur in the park. There are reports of specific attacks on families, especially when members are caught alone. The main culprit is always described as a large six-foot-plus hefty male wearing a black ski mask and carrying a wooden baseball bat. City officials have put out a warning to the refugees never to wander alone but always in small groups, especially families.

We think the assailant is one of those "singles" with a grudge against families and their preferential treatment. "Grudge," as we call him, hasn't killed anyone yet, though he's put one adult male and two teenaged boys in the hospital and has threatened several females with sexual assault, without, so far, carrying out his threats. But the attacks and threats are occurring with greater frequency and we fear it's only a matter of time before he kills or rapes someone. We've been put on special alert—especially since Grudge likes to strike at night.

Thursday rounds begin as normal. Nedda and I start in section 32 and work our way east. There are a few groups of people milling about on the sidewalks—likely teens hanging out. Then I spy them—a small group of three, one tall male and two smaller females, one possibly a young child—being threatened by a huge bulk of a man carrying a baseball bat. Their body auras are bright, reflecting the heat given off by extreme emotions.

"Michelle!" I shout. "I think I've got him! Grudge. Section 34, corners A3 and DF."

I hear Michelle shift in her seat next to me. "Hunter is five blocks away, but we're coming."

My heart begins to pound as Grudge grabs the tall man by the shirt and starts yelling in his face. The two girls scream as Nedda circles above, just out of sight of those on the ground. With a sudden thrust, Grudge pushes the other man away and raises his baseball bat.

"Michelle!" I shout.

"Two blocks!" she shouts back. "Can you hold him?"

Hold him? With Nedda? Grudge swings the bat and the tall man ducks, raising his arm to ward off the blow. There is a loud crack, and the tall man staggers back and collapses to his knees, his left arm dangling limp. Again the girls scream, the larger one holding the other. Nedda circles frantically, sensing my alarm. Grudge raises his bat for the kill, and I give Nedda the command. She swoops down, beating her wings against Grudge's face, darting for his eyes with her small snout. Grudge drops his bat, arms flailing, his cries of fear echoing loudly in Nedda's ears.

"Almost there!" Michelle says, and I faintly discern the running patter of Hunter's feet.

Then Grudge's large fist hammers into Nedda. Pain explodes in my head and everything goes dark. Silent. "Nedda!" I cry and I am back in my seat at the Command Center. I've lost my empath connection. A strange dizziness envelopes me, and I black out.

Two days later, I visit Nedda in the animal infirmary. Grudge's blow broke her right wing and damaged both her implant and the echolocation center of her brain. Nedda is as blind as I am now. I've been assured that she will be retired to live out the rest of her 6-8 years feasting on hand-fed insects and being pampered by caretakers in the AHEP retirement facilities. Often children are allowed to visit decommissioned animal empaths. Other times the empaths are taken to nursing homes for the residents to interact with—provided the empath's mental and emotional stability is confirmed. I wonder how well a bat will be received.

I sit and stroke Nedda, careful not to disturb her bandaged wing. She nestles against my left arm in her usual spot, contented just to be near me and my scent. My emotions range from sorrow over Nedda's condition to gratefulness that she still lives to satisfaction upon learning that Grudge is awaiting sentencing for both his attacks on the refugees and on Nedda—and recovering with 47 stitches where Hunter tore into his face. Both Hunter and Nedda have been given special commendations. And the father, arm in a cast, and his two daughters have already made plans to visit both their rescuers.

I hear a rustle near me and Dr. MacKenzie lays one hand on my shoulder. "You have a brave little friend there," she says. "She'll be alright. Tomorrow, you start training with a new partner."

"Another bat?" I ask.

"Another bat," she replies.

I nod, but I'm not happy. No one can replace Nedda.

*   *   *   *

Once again I find myself seated in an overly padded chair in the Receiving Room. I lean my head forward to free my ears from the headrest. The door opens and I hear two sets of footsteps enter. "Good morning, Officer Beckworth," Dr. MacKenzie says brightly.

"Ma'am," I say.

"We have your new partner. Lt. Rimon will place her in your lap now."

Another female bat? I lick my lips and sit still as a small body is placed on my thighs.

"She's already received her implant chip using the same frequency as Nedda. You should be able to connect fairly easily."

I nod, but say nothing. I'm not sure I want to connect with this strange creature. It's not easy letting go of a previous bonding. Nedda means too much to me. I'm still mourning over our severed empathy.

Lt. Rimon understands. "We'll leave you two to get acquainted," he says in his raspy voice. "Good luck."

The footsteps turn to leave, but one set hesitates. "Just for your information," Dr. MacKenzie says, "little Pixie there is Nedda's younger sister." The door closes.

Pixie. Nedda's sister. As I process this bit of information, I reflexively move my right hand to start stroking Pixie's back with my forefinger. Pixie settles against my left arm in that same contented mode Nedda has, reminding me of a cat purring. Pixie is smaller than Nedda, but she has the same soft fur, leathery wings, and tiny pointed ears. My thoughts drift as I continue stroking Pixie's back. Then I feel it, that strange sensation cascading down from my neck to the small of my back as I sense my finger on Pixie's fur. Slowly, a faint orange-yellow glow begins to flicker in my mind as the Receiving Room comes into focus. I hear soft whispers in the hall beyond the closed door. Probably Dr. MacKenzie and Lt. Rimon wondering how I'm doing. And I smell Pixie's warm musty scent as she nestles in my lap.

I smile. "Hello, Pixie," I whisper. Then I lean back in my chair—and start to fly.

Powers That Be

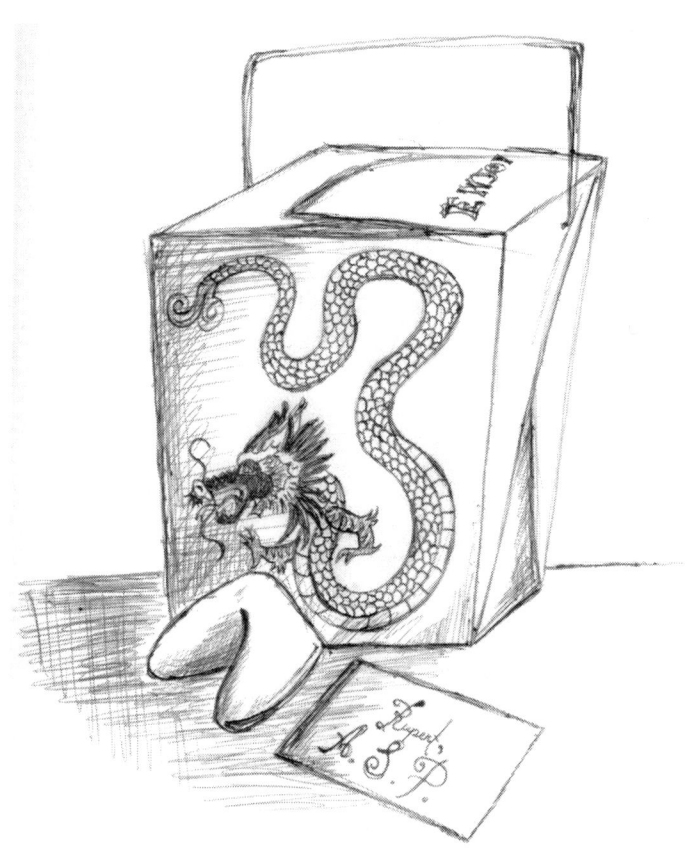

By Silver and Fire
By B. David Spicer

I have struggled to understand the events of the last several weeks, but my mind, a thing for which I was once exceptionally proud, has failed the task and I am left utterly at a loss. Most who know me describe me as a rational man, a devotee of logic and science. I am not prone to flights of fancy or quick to accept anything that cannot be empirically proven. That said, I now set pen to paper, not as a rational man noting a rational event, for what I've seen defies reason, but as a man recording for posterity events that are absolutely beyond explanation.

It started in the spring, when my wife, dearest Elizabeth, succumbed to pneumonia after months of being bedridden; she struggled bravely until the end. When she loosened her tenuous hold on life, and her hand fell from my own, I can scarcely describe the black morass that I fell into. My beloved had departed, and I remained behind, in unspeakable anguish. I clutched her to me and held her until I could weep no more.

If I'd been a weaker man, I admit that I might have done something drastic, and old Ryman, my devoted servant, watched me closely lest I tumble too deeply

41

into my inner misery and tie a noose or load a pistol. Ryman's vigil, though well intentioned, was not necessary. Yes, my soul lingered in the deepest despair and it seemed that I might never recover, but I had Elise to consider. Though her mother had left us before her time, my daughter, a burgeoning eight- year-old bundle of breathless energy, remained.

Elise's hair gleamed like burnished copper, a trait she inherited from her mother's Irish ancestors, though her brown eyes came from my sensible English forebears. My own grief, monstrous in its intensity, paled compared to the abyss that swallowed my daughter. Relatives, cousins and aunts who had brought upon her paroxysms of joy previously, received from her only cold, tearless silence. Elise stared at her mother's mortal remains from across the room and steadfastly ignored consolation from anyone. She didn't speak, she didn't wail in misery, and she shed not one tear. Instead, she fell away, retreating into the innermost reaches of the human psyche.

Rev. McCallum patted me on the shoulder. "She'll get over it. It's just been a shock. Give her some time."

I nodded. "Yes, I hope you're right, Reverend. It's been quite a shock to all of us."

The morning of the funeral I went to Elise's room. Liddy, the governess, had dressed my daughter in a somber black outfit. She stood there, solemn and silent, with cold, distant eyes that seemed more dead than alive. I knelt in front of her and took both of her hands into my own.

"Good morning, Elise."

She stared through me as if I weren't in the room with her.

"I know you miss your mama, I miss her as well, terribly so. I know how much you hurt because I hurt that much as well." I touched her chest. "In here, where it hurts now, later you'll remember your mama, and the pain will be replaced by good feelings. Do you believe me?"

She didn't acknowledge me. Her eyes focused on some point behind me, not outside the house, but some distant speck in another world.

I gave her hands a little squeeze. "Well, I know it seems impossible to believe right now, but it's true. Your mother will always be with you, Elise, in your heart and in your soul. Do you believe that at least?"

I waited, trying desperately to catch her eye, to make her see me. She stood there like a rag doll, evincing the same lifeless spirit a rag doll has. I gave her a hug, which she didn't return, and stood. I hung my head for a moment, wondering what she was thinking and trying to decipher the cause of her continued silence. I stepped into the hall with Liddy.

"She blames me, Liddy. It's as if she thinks I murdered her mother." I covered my face to hide my brimming eyes.

Liddy clucked her tongue. "Not at all, sir. She's just terribly upset by her mother's passing. She'll come around in a few days' time."

I looked Liddy, square in the face. "So, you consider this normal behavior?"

She bit her lip. "Well, no, sir. She's taken the death harder than most, that's all."

I nodded. "I'm sorry, Liddy. I'm quite upset, and I'm forgetting my manners. Elise just needs some time. You're quite right."

"Indeed, sir."

The gathering at the cemetery included relatives from as far away as Cornwall and one elderly great-aunt from Caithness. My dear wife's passing had summoned mourners from all over Britain, and while I appreciated their collective presence, only one mourner really mattered to me. Elise stood in her mourning dress, stoic and stoney-faced, watching her mother's casket being lowered into the grave. Where were her tears? Why had none fallen? Weeping, wailing, thrashing about—those were the normal reactions to death, all of which I had seen with my own eyes. Not from Elise, however. I began to feel a deep unease, but I couldn't understand why.

Despite the oft-repeated admonition, "She just needs time," Elise's distemper did not improve. She became a hollow child, devoid of the burning energy she had displayed in earlier times. She still refused to speak, ignoring any attempt at communication. She would eat only when directed to do so, a mechanical process of stuffing food into her mouth, chewing briefly and swallowing it nearly whole. She evinced no joy in eating, even when her favorite dishes were set before her, and she clearly began to lose weight. She sat in her darkened bedroom, in her mother's rocking chair, staring at, but not out of, the window.

Of course, my concern for my daughter quickly became acute, and I summoned doctors, so many doctors, but each claimed that Elise's condition was temporary and that, given enough time, she would make a full recovery. Time, that's what she needed, but as I watched her waste away before my eyes, it became clear that time was just what Elise didn't have.

Liddy suggested a trip abroad, to Paris or Geneva, possibly even America, and she expressed an admirable facsimile of certainty that such a change of scenery would shake little Elise out of her depression. Ryman had a similar idea, but one that I liked much better. He suggested we relocate the household to my country house in Devonshire, near the village of Grimpen. There, in the village, were many young girls near in age to Elise with whom she could romp through the garden and wood. I decided it right then, and we began packing for the trip that very night.

We journeyed south by rail, and I hoped that this relatively novel experience would elicit some reaction from Elise, but she spent the trip staring at her feet, resolutely disinterested in the panorama beyond the window pane. From the train station we hired a pair of carriages to convey us to my estate, a matter of some ten miles. We passed through the town of Grimpen and were halted on the road by a large flock of sheep. I pointed out the wooly beasts to my daughter, who regarded them with no interest. She closed her eyes and spent the remainder of the trip asleep.

Greymoor Hall, my family's seat in Devonshire for two centuries, sat on a low moor bordered by a stretch of woodland on one side and a stinking mire on the other. Despite its somewhat grandiose name, Greymoor Hall was a great drafty, tumbledown house always in need of some manner of repair and could be described, generously, as ugly. Elizabeth had loved the place though, and my favorite memories of it all had Elizabeth in them. Elise had only been there once before but her love of it rivaled even her mother's. Her laughter had echoed through the house then, and I admit to straining my ears to catch that echo, for I desperately wished to hear it again.

Campbell, the groundskeeper, met us at the gate. He took off his hat and bowed his bald head in my direction. "Sir Warren, you'll find everything just as you left it."

I clapped him on the shoulder. "I hope you're right, because I left a great deal of happiness here when I last left, and I hope to find some of it now that I've returned."

Campbell nodded slowly. "I heard about the lady. I was mighty sorry to hear she passed. Mighty sorry indeed." He looked down at Elise, who stood next to me, her hand in mine. "Hello, little miss. Do you remember me?" He gave her a wide toothless grin, but she continued gazing at some vague spot on the ground before her. He waited but she didn't speak. "Ah, well, perhaps we'll talk later." He shot me a sympathetic look and we moved up the path to the house.

Liddy and Ryman, assisted by a troop of housekeepers brought from the village, uncovered furniture and unpacked luggage. I took Elise into the library, where I stood perusing the titles of the leather-bound tomes that my father had brought to the house. Elise, much to my surprise, crossed the room and curled up in the window seat with her knees drawn up to her chin. She stared listlessly out the window, but even this small action was such a vast improvement that I dared not speak a word. I stood motionless, watching her, when I felt the years roll back and I saw a younger Elise sitting in that very same seat, in that very same posture, with her mother seated across from her, reading fairy tales aloud. It became clear to me then, she had taken that particular seat because she had once shared it with her mother. The fathomless depths of my daughter's pain, so clearly displayed in that window seat, stung my eyes and put a lump in my throat.

Even such a small thing as my daughter moving to take a seat in the window on her own volition constituted a victory, and over the next few days we celebrated more victories. One bright morning Liddy took Elise by carriage into Grimpen, where young Niles Frankland, the nephew of a neighbor on the moor, was walking with his dogs, a brace of terriers. Elise knelt to scratch the dogs behind their ears, and they rewarded her by lapping her face with their little pink tongues. And Elise smiled.

"She smiled?" I sat down behind my desk and stared at Liddy. "You're sure?"

"Definitely, sir." Liddy smiled then. "Young Master Frankland was about to move on, but I took him by the elbow and bade him to wait a moment. I'm sure he didn't see the importance of a child being tickled by a dog's tongue, but he waited until the dogs had finished with Elise before moving on. I tell you, Sir Warren, I haven't seen a smile on Elise's face since before her mother's passing. I nearly wept for joy! Of course, she sneezed all the way home, as she always does after petting a dog, but even that could not erase her smile."

I laughed. "If it weren't for the sneezing, I'd buy her a dozen hounds!"

Over the weeks since the funeral, Elise had eaten very little, and coercing her to eat had become a nightly problem yet to be properly solved. The child had withered to a rattling skeleton wearing the costume of a little girl. Her eyes had sunken into bruised pits within her skull and lost any semblance of life. The day that she had patted Master Frankland's dogs, however, she ate

47

everything on her plate without the constant admonition to do so.

A few days later, Ryman approached me in the garden. "Might I have a word with you, sir?"

"Of course, Ryman. What is it?"

"Well, sir, I have something to tell you about your daughter."

That got my attention. "Please, go on."

"You remember sir, last night I came to tell you about the horse coming up lame?"

"Certainly."

"Well sir, after I left your bedchamber I passed the door to miss Elise's room."

I nodded. "Naturally."

"I heard something." He twisted his cap in his gnarled hands. "I heard talking."

"Talking?"

"Yes, sir. Your daughter was speaking."

I took him by the shoulders in my excitement. "She spoke? That is excellent news, old friend!"

"Ah, yes, sir." He cleared his throat. "But sir, I heard *two* voices coming from the room."

"Two voices? Who else was in the room? Liddy?"

He twisted his cap into a knot of gray wool. "That's just it, sir, I couldn't place the other voice. It was definitely not Liddy's voice. It sounded, ah, harsh, sir, like an old man's voice."

I rubbed my furrowed brow. "Could it have been Campbell? Though why he'd have been in Elise's room is beyond me."

Ryman shook his head. "No sir, Campbell had gone into Grimpen to have dinner with his sister. I saw him come through the gate at half-past eleven."

I ran down the list of servants in the household. Besides Ryman and Campbell, the only males in my employ were the gardener, a young man named Lewis who lived in Grimpen, and Liddy's nephew Giles who worked as a stable boy. He was only fourteen, and his voice could hardly be described as harsh. I shook my head. "What did she say?"

"I couldn't hear much through the door, but I thought she might have been talking about pie. And tea."

I smiled and clapped Ryman on the shoulder. "There you go, Ryman. Elise must have been playing with her dolls, having a tea party. I've watched her play that game before. She would ask her dolls questions like, 'Do you want more tea, Alice,' and she would answer, 'Yes, please,' in Alice's voice. That, Ryman, is undoubtedly what you heard. It warms my soul to hear that she's speaking again, even if it's to a doll." That was the rational answer my mind settled upon.

He nodded slowly. "Yes, sir, I admit that's possible, but what about the harsh voice? Would your daughter speak with such a voice during her play?"

"Perhaps her doll has a cold?" I laughed heartily, and after a moment Ryman joined me.

"Very good, sir."

As he walked away, Ryman shook his head slowly, and I got the distinct impression that he didn't quite accept my explanation of what he had heard through the door. I hadn't heard Elise speak a single word since her mother's passing, so Ryman's description of the event failed to make the proper impression upon me. Looking back, instead of elation, I should have felt deeply uneasy, and I should have taken Ryman at his word. The

49

man had been with my family for decades, and I had just dismissed his concern for my daughter as a misheard tea party because it was the logical thing to do.

That night, I tucked Elise into her bed and wished her goodnight. She turned to look at me and smiled. "Goodnight, Papa."

My heart skipped a beat. She had spoken! I kissed her brow, closed the door and retreated to the library where I sat in the window seat, placed my hands over my eyes and wept like a baby. My child had spoken! To me! My heart soared with the hope that Elise had returned to me from whatever distant mental redoubt she had taken refuge in. I felt, in that moment, happier than I had in months, since before Elizabeth's illness.

As I sat alternatively weeping and smiling in the darkness, I discerned footsteps in the hall, the quickstepping patter of a child's footfall. I stumbled to my desk and lit a lamp. I opened the library door and peered down the darkened hall. I saw nobody. "Elise?" No voice responded, but I heard a quick intake of breath, the sort of sound one makes when they are taken by surprise. I frowned as I squinted into the dimness. "Elise, is that you? Are playing a trick on your poor papa?"

I turned up the wick in my lamp for more light, followed the length of the hall and entered the dining room. The hairs on the back of my neck stood as a chill raced down my spine. I felt quite clearly that someone was watching me. I lowered the lamp and searched under the table, where I found nothing. While my head was hidden beneath the dangling edge of the tablecloth I heard more patter on the floorboards. I stood up quickly, spinning around and squinting into shadows. "Elise? Is that you?"

For a moment I heard nothing, then I heard a small voice, small but horrifying in its inhuman intonation.

"Not Elise."

I froze in place, my heart nearly stopping its beat. My hands trembled, causing the lamp's flame to dance on the wick. I heard a quick chuckle from behind me, followed by childlike footsteps dashing through the kitchen and up the back stairs. I took a deep breath to steady my nerves before I also climbed the back stairs. I ascended slowly, carefully, quietly. The second floor hallway was dark and deserted.

I stepped toward Elise's bedroom and found the door ajar. I pushed it open and stood beside her bed. Her eyes danced beneath their eyelids and her breath came and went in the slowly regular pace of sleep. I brushed a lock of hair from her forehead. She didn't move. I knelt to kiss her cheek. "I love you, Elise." I started toward the door again when I heard that grotesquely savage voice again.

"Not Elise."

I whirled, my eyes slashing across the darkened room, searching for the source of those ghastly words. Try as I might, I could see nothing out of place, no bogeyman beneath the bed, only my beautiful daughter sleeping the sleep of the just. I remembered Ryman's words then, his description of the harsh voice, and I became very afraid. Not afraid that some ghost haunted the house, but rather that my beloved daughter's mind had become disarranged by the death of her mother. I feared that that inhuman voice was just a twisted parody of Elise's own. That thought terrified me more than I can describe. I went to bed then, but sleep didn't find me that night.

I spent the night brooding but came to no clear decision. That morning I felt like a black cloud hung over me as I dressed and descended the stairs for breakfast. The strange voice I'd heard in both the dining room and in Elise's bedroom reverberated through my mind. Could that sound really have come from my daughter's throat? If so, what did that imply about her mental state? My resolute scowl fell off of my face when I approached the breakfast table.

Elise sat in her chair shoveling waffles, a Continental food her mother always had for breakfast, into her mouth with gusto. I felt my jaw swing open, and I stood there, unmoving, watching her eat. Liddy drew up beside me. "I'm sorry sir, she asked if she could start eating right away because she was quite hungry. She surprised me by speaking at all, and well, she could do with a good meal."

I placed a hand on her shoulder, but it took a minute before I could speak around the lump in my throat. "You were quite right to let her eat." I found a smile and tried it on, glad to see that it still fit. "Liddy, I think she's coming out of it, her despair I mean. I think she's going to be all right."

Liddy's mouth drew together in a wrinkled pucker, a sure sign that she had something unpleasant to say. I took her by the elbow and led her into the hall. "What is it Liddy?"

She swallowed hard before speaking. "Mrs. Burns told me this morning that a mincemeat pie she had made yesterday has come up missing. She said she put it in the pantry before she retired for the evening."

"Missing? A whole pie?"

Liddy nodded. "Yes, sir." She chewed her lower lip. "There's more to the story?"

"Yes, sir." She led me to the kitchen where she indicated a pie pan that held the crumbling remains of a mincemeat pie. "I found this in Elise's room this morning, when I went in to wake her."

The pie looked as if it had been eaten from the top down, the lower crust still clung to the bottom of the pan. "She ate a whole pie? By herself?"

"That's my belief, sir."

I'm not certain how Liddy expected me to react, with anger perhaps, but when I burst into laughter, her eyebrows rose and her mouth opened into a gaping "O."

"Tell Mrs. Burns to make another pie. If Elise has found her appetite, I won't begrudge her a pie."

"Yes, sir. There is just one other thing. Campbell has asked to speak with you and Ryman, once you've breakfasted."

"Very well." Elise burst into the kitchen, followed by Mrs. Burns. The smile on Elise's face, so long absent, was now almost painful to see. I knelt down to face her. "Good morning Elise."

She threw herself at me, hugging me to her. "Good morning, Papa!"

"I see you've already eaten."

"Yes, Papa! I was so hungry!"

I smiled at her. "You were? Even after eating a mincemeat pie last night?"

She laughed, a lilting ballet of sound. "I didn't eat the pie, Papa!"

"You didn't?" I shot a glance at Liddy, whose mouth had puckered up again. "Well, who did?"

53

"That was Gorham. He ate the pie!" She laughed again.

"Gorham? Who's that? Is he your friend?"

She nodded vigorously. "Yes! He's so funny!" She giggled and twisted a blonde lock around a tiny finger.

"Does he have a funny, scratchy voice?"

Her eyes widened and she laughed again. "Yes! Have you seen him? He said nobody would, because he was good at hiding."

"No, I haven't seen him. He must really be good at hiding if nobody can see him."

She hugged me again. "Papa, may I go play in the garden?"

"Of course, darling. Have fun."

"Thank you, Papa!" She dashed out through the kitchen door and raced across the lawn.

I stood, and couldn't help smiling. "The change in her behavior, it's almost miraculous." I turned to Mrs. Burns. "How much did she eat?"

The cook chuckled. "On my honor, sir, I've never seen a child eat so much at one sitting. She ate six large waffles! If I may say so, sir, she could have done with six more. There's not much meat left on that poor child."

I nodded. "Yes, she's eaten so little since . . . since the funeral. But to eat an entire mincemeat pie in the middle of the night, and six waffles just a few hours later? Where is she putting it?"

Liddy cleared her throat. "What do you make of this 'Gorham' character, sir?"

"That is an interesting question." I rubbed my chin with my fingertips. "He's clearly an imaginary friend of some sort." A logical assumption.

"What are we to do about him, sir?" Liddy didn't seem to like the idea of Elise's new friend. "It doesn't feel right."

"It is a strange development, I'll agree with you, Liddy, but look at Elise now. She's speaking, she's eating, she's playing."

"She's stealing."

That made me laugh. "I'm willing to indulge her imaginary friend, for a while anyway. If this Gorham figure is responsible for her improved mood, I'll pin a medal on his invisible chest. I think I heard her speak in a strange voice last night, and I take it that was supposed to be Gorham's voice." I watched her smelling the roses in the garden. "Gorham is welcome here. For now."

I could see that Liddy disagreed, but she didn't say so. "Very good, sir."

I turned to Mrs. Burns again. "Did Elise leave any waffles for me?"

Ryman, Campbell and the gardener, Lewis, stood in a knot near the chicken house. I strode across the lawn toward them, and I could see Elise in the garden, leaping from flagstone to flagstone on the edge of the graveled pathway. The men stopped talking as I approached. "Good morning, fellows. Liddy told me you needed to speak with me."

Campbell nodded and cleared his throat before continuing. "Yes, sir. We've found something, ah, strange, sir. Lewis found it this morning."

I looked at each of them in turn. "Something strange? Can you be more specific?"

"Perhaps you should just see it for yourself, sir." Campbell led me to the far side of the chicken house and gestured to the burned carcass of a hen. Strange squiggles painted in chicken-blood decorated the side of the chicken house, above the carcass.

I knelt and examined the bird. It's head had been removed, while the rest was badly mutilated. The whole mess had been burned in a small fire. The markings on the wall were crude and meant nothing to me. "What am I looking at? Who did this?"

The three men looked at each other. Campbell shook his head slowly. "We aren't sure, sir, in any specific sort of way." He licked his lips, reluctant to continue. "But Lewis says he's heard of such things." He stepped aside and indicated the young Grimpen man with a gesture.

"Mr. Lewis?" I stood and gave him my eye. "You know something about this?"

"Well, sir, you see, my gran' used to tell of such things, of symbols painted in blood and burned carcasses. She used to tell stories of them what followed the old ways, sir. The fire, sir, that's rowan wood, sure enough."

He stopped speaking, clearly thinking he'd made himself clear. "Rowan wood?"

Lewis nodded enthusiastically. "Yes, sir. Without a doubt."

I poked my finger through the ashes and picked up a bit up burned wood. "What old ways are you talking about?"

"He means witches, Sir Warren." Ryman pointed to the crimson symbols. "He means this is a hex of some kind, isn't that so, Lewis?"

"Well, now I couldn't speak as to it being a hex or not, but it is magic." He paused for a moment and looked up at me. "Black magic, sir. That's always worked with blood."

I watched the three of them for a minute, wondering if this could be a colossal joke, but they all remained grim. "Lewis, wipe that writing off the wall and bury the rest of it."

"Yes, sir." He set off to find a shovel.

I turned to Campbell. "Who has a key to the chicken house?"

"I have the only one, save the one on the master key-ring." He rubbed at his forehead nervously. "You're wondering how somebody got a chicken after dark?"

"Yes, that thought had crossed my mind. The only other way into the chicken house is through the hen-door, which is much too small for anybody to crawl through."

Ryman shook his head. "No sir, a child might fit through the hen-door."

"A child?" I turned to Campbell. "Do you think a child would fit through the hen-door?"

He rolled it around through his mind for a minute. "I believe so, sir, but it would have to be a very small child."

"Miss Elise would fit." Ryman had his hands in his pockets and his eyes on the ground.

Silence, uncomfortable and thick hung between us for several moments. Finally I spoke. "Ryman, my daughter is not in the habit of killing chickens and throwing hexes about."

"Has she been in the habit of stealing mincemeat pies, in times past?" He finally met my eye. "Liddy told me about that this morning."

My voice came out sharper than I'd intended. "Just what are you getting at, Ryman?"

He held my gaze, his own never wavering. "I fear for the child, sir. Now, more than ever."

"Now? She's improved greatly in just a few days, Ryman. Why would you fear for her now?"

"The voice, sir, that I heard in her bedroom. I swear to you, sir, it was not human! If you'd heard it with your own ears, you'd understand my concern."

I looked away, toward the garden, but didn't see Elise. "I heard it, Ryman. Last night."

His eyes widened and he licked his lips. "You did? So, you must see that something terrible has happened. Something evil has attached itself to Miss Elise."

"No, Ryman, not at all. Elise has created an imaginary friend, a boy named Gorham. She twists her own voice terribly to approximate his voice, I'll admit that. She claims that Gorham ate the pie."

"A lie? She lied to you?"

Dear old Campbell felt just then he had to defend Elise. "Now just a moment, Ryman. . ."

"I mean no disrespect, Sir Warren, but when she says that this Gorham chap ate the pie, she is in fact telling you an untruth." I'd never seen Ryman so upset. Usually he was the definition of unflappable English aplomb. "I've never known Miss Elise to tell lies before . . ."

"Before her mother died?" I nodded and gripped his arm. "Ryman, please understand, when her mother died, my daughter's mind fell to a very dark and lonely place. What she needed was a friend, one true friend, to lead her out of the pit of despair and into the sunshine again. So she created Gorham for that purpose. Her recovery has begun, but it's not complete. When she no longer needs Gorham, we'll find that he has run away, or that a sparrow has snatched him up in its beak. Her behavior will return to normal, but it will take time. Grieving is an empirically proven process that takes time to work through."

Ryman stood up straight. "As you say, sir. If that's all, I shall resume my duties." When I nodded he turned around and headed toward the house.

We watched him enter the house through the kitchen door. "He's spooked." Campbell scratched his stubbly chin. "That's not like Ryman."

I watched him close the door behind him. "No, Campbell, it isn't like him at all."

"Do you suppose he really thinks your daughter killed the chicken?"

"He didn't come right out and say it, but I think he believes that she did." I turned to face Campbell. "I must admit, there are some strange things afoot. If Elise did kill a chicken, or rather if Gorham killed it, we might have a more serious problem than I'd thought."

"Perhaps you should call in a doctor? Dr. Mortimer lives in Grimpen."

I chuckled. "I doubt the local practitioners have much grasp of disarranged minds."

"Dr. Mortimer is an older man, sir. He spent most of his younger days practicing medicine in London. He's quite an intelligent man, a man of science, or so I've been told. It couldn't hurt to ask his opinion."

I had to admit, that sounded promising. "In that case, Campbell, invite him to dinner tomorrow. We'll give him the chance to watch Elise without her suspecting anything."

"Very good, sir." He left to attend to that duty, and I turned my feet toward the garden. I couldn't see Elise, so I followed the gravel path amongst the plants. The roses were in bloom, but as I stopped to admire them, I noticed that the blooms on the lower reaches of the vine had been torn apart. The red petals were crushed and stomped into the ground. I knelt to examine the situation when I heard Elise's voice on the far side of the hedge.

"Gorham! Flowers aren't meant to be stepped on!" She laughed merrily.

"Why?" Gorham's voice answered. "Taste bad. Smell bad." I could hear the rustle of vines and harsh, stentorian breathing. "Hate them! Hate them! Hate them!" The rustling increased, sounding like a strong man was hauling out the rosebush by the roots. "Hate them! Hate them!" Then I heard a snuffling sound followed by a coughing grunt and the swift patter of feet crunching on the gravel.

I hurried around the hedge and found Elise sitting on a stone bench, swinging her feet and humming a happy little tune. She smiled when she saw me. "Hello, Papa!"

"Hello, Elise. What happened to the flowers?" I gestured to the ruined rosebush.

She gave it a quick glance, then laughed. "I don't think Gorham likes flowers."

"So I see." The bush was destroyed, and strangely, almost completely uprooted. I doubted I could have pulled it out of the ground so completely. "Campbell won't be happy to see what you've done to his roses, Elise." I watched her closely to see how she'd react.

"I didn't do it, Papa! It was Gorham!" Her little face took on a pleading expression. "Really, Papa! It was Gorham!"

"It was Gorham, was it?"

"Yes, Papa! See?" She held out her hands, which were perfectly clean. My brows furrowed as I looked her over. If she'd been working at the rosebush, pulling at it with some reserve of manic strength, she couldn't have helped getting herself dirty, but her feet, her knees, her dress were all still clean. She pouted a little. "You don't believe me?"

"Of course I do. Please tell Gorham to stop uprooting the flowers though." I gave her a kiss and she giggled.

"I'll tell him!" With that, she ran toward the house, while I sat on the bench regarding the crumpled rosebush.

"How could she have pulled that bush out of the ground?" I raised my eyes to the sky. "Elizabeth, my dear, I need your help. I don't understand what's happening here." Elizabeth didn't answer, but a cloud danced in front of the sun in just that moment, leaving me feeling confused and lonely.

The following morning brought reports from Mrs. Burns, who found a five pound wheel of cheese missing from the pantry, and from Liddy, who found strange ashes on various windowsills and lintels. Campbell found evidence of a small bonfire on the garden path, rowan wood again. My mind whirled and my appetite fled. Elise, however, ate a hearty breakfast before going to the stables with Campbell for a pony ride.

"I don't understand any of this!" I tossed aside my breakfast. "What is going on in this house!"

Ryman stood uncertainly beside the table. "I cannot say, Sir Warren."

61

"I have wheels of cheese coming up missing, fires being set on the lawn! It makes no sense at all." I threw up my hands in exasperation. "Who can eat five pounds of cheese in a night?"

"Something unnatural." Ryman stood stiffly, with his eyes staring out the window. I followed his gaze and found my daughter.

Before I could ask what he meant, Liddy entered the room with a letter. She handed it to me and I absently tore it open. "Well, here's some good news at last! Dr. Mortimer has consented to come to dinner tonight and consult with us concerning Elise."

"And Gorham?" Ryman still didn't look at me.

"Yes, I suppose." I turned to Liddy. "Have Mrs. Burns prepare something extra special, that is, if Gorham hasn't eaten everything in the pantry."

Dr. Mortimer turned out to be a robust man with a ruddy complexion and boisterous booming voice. He laughed loudly and often and fell to his supper with obvious enthusiasm. His eyes were bright and quick, and seemed to miss very little. Indeed, when we'd finished our meal and adjourned to the library for cigars and brandy, he seemed already to know much of our troubles.

"Well, Sir Warren, let's get to it, shall we? You are having a problem with your daughter?"

I nodded as I set my cigar alight. "Yes, that's true Dr. Mortimer."

"You've recently lost your wife? Within the last month or two?"

"Indeed. Are you a wizard, sir?"

He chuckled around his cigar. "No, Sir Warren, nothing of the sort. In the hall hangs a portrait of a young woman, still shrouded in black. Since you studiously avoided speaking of your wife during dinner, I assumed that the portrait was of her." He took a great puff of his cigar. "A colleague of mine displays a wonderful talent for noticing small details and making great mental leaps based on his observations. Compared to him, I am a rank amateur. Now then, Please fill me in on what has been happening with your daughter."

So I did, starting with Elizabeth's death and Elise's withering into herself, Gorham's appearance and the strange things that accompanied it. He listened carefully, asking no questions but puffing rigorously on his cigar. After I finished, he sat motionless in his chair for several minutes before he spoke. "You, Sir Warren, have a problem. Actually, two problems."

"Two?"

"That's right, two. The first concerns your daughter's mental state, the second concerns the mental state of some other person in your household." He stood to refill his brandy glass. "As you stated, your wife's passing caused your poor daughter to retreat deep into her own mind, a place where she felt safe. That she has returned from that mental abyss can only be a good sign, but the appearance of this Gorham creature and the associated thefts, well, that is a not-so-good sign."

"Yes, I agree." I refilled my own glass. "I had assumed that her need for this imaginary friend would eventually disappear and he with it."

Dr. Mortimer nodded vigorously. "Oh yes, that's certainly how such things normally work. Imaginary friends seldom remain for more than a few years, that's a few years at most—often they go away after a few mere

63

months." He puffed away at his cigar, his eyes growing distant.

"Then the best course is to simply let things proceed without taking any action?"

He shook himself, looking almost as if he'd just woken up. "In this case, no."

"No?"

"No, Sir Warren, no. As I indicated, you have two problems, and I don't think you can wait long to solve the second."

"Please continue, doctor."

"Your daughter's derangement has been noticed by the household staff?"

I nodded. "Yes, by now I'm certain that they've all heard everything there is to hear. Why do you ask?"

"The fires and the chicken. The ashes and the writing on the chicken house wall. These are attempts at magic, Sir Warren."

"Magic? My gardener believes that as well, but as you and I are rational men, we know that magic is just a myth, as are elves and fairies. Just fantasies held by the uneducated." I waved my hand to dismiss the absurdity.

"It is magic." Dr. Mortimer mashed his cigar out in the ashtray. "I am quite serious."

"Nonsense, doctor. Magic is just humbug."

"Indeed." He chuckled. "Perhaps I chose the word poorly. Whoever is killing chickens and writing on walls in blood is practicing a belief, one different from the beliefs we both hold, and to them, magic is not humbug. Magic is a real force in the world, and there is more magic in the world than either of us can fathom."

I sat for several minutes, turning over this revelation. "Why is this person working a spell here? Why now?"

"I suspect that he—or she—is afraid."

"Of what?"

"Your daughter." He locked his eyes on mine. "Her strange behavior, likely the strange voice that she uses when speaking for Gorham, has frightened someone. Perhaps they believe she is possessed by an evil spirit. The ashes on the window sills and doorways, which are points of entry, imply a desire to keep something out of the house. Take that for what you will—I make no claim to be versed in the ways of magic."

When I spoke, my voice sounded louder than I had intended. "Dr. Mortimer, my daughter is not possessed by an evil spirit, the devil, or even by Queen Victoria herself!"

He didn't seem offended. "I never said that she was, simply that someone in this household seems to think that she is, which is an infinitely more dangerous situation. If she is allowed to persist with this imaginary friend nonsense, I fear that the actions of our unknown magician will become ever more desperate, and possibly quite dangerous."

I stood and crossed the room, staring through the window into the darkness beyond. "What shall I do? Return with Elise to London?"

"I wouldn't advise that. Her recovery began when you brought her here; therefore, it seems likely that this place, or the memories within it, are what triggered her recovery. I would think that her mind is in a precarious state of recovery and that returning to the city could send her back into the darkness."

65

"I see. What do you suggest? Firing the staff?"

"Well, that could also upset the apple cart, just as much as returning to London. By accident you've hit upon a situation that benefits the girl's recovery. Changing anything, such as letting the staff go, could be detrimental. As I understand it, most of your help is from Grimpen, is that right?"

"Most of them, yes. Ryman is from Kent originally, and Liddy and her nephew are from Inverness. Campbell, Lewis, Mrs. Burns and the housemaids are from Grimpen."

He nodded. "I thought as much. Here, on these dreary moors, magic seems to be found in every tree, in every rock, in every badger and hound. I think the best solution is to disabuse young Elise of the notion that Gorham is a real person. Once that is achieved, the need for protective magic will vanish. Get rid of Gorham, and your magician will stop killing your chickens."

He went on to suggest confronting Elise whilst Gorham was supposedly present, thus forcing her to acknowledge her imaginary friend's unreality. Just before he left, Dr. Mortimer paused and turned to me. "Understand that Gorham fulfills some need for your daughter, and that she might not be willing to let him go. You must weigh the benefits of allowing her to continue with her fantasy against the danger presented by your unknown adversary."

I spent a few days considering what to do, and in that time, Lewis found two more chickens burned in rowan-wood fires, and most ominously, more bloody symbols were written, but on the main house this time. A venison roast, two apple tarts, and a sack of walnuts also came up missing. Mrs. Burns became so upset by these events that she very nearly resigned her position; two of the housemaids did just that. I was running out of time.

My plan for confronting Elise, I must admit, could best be described as crude. I concealed myself in the closet of Elise's bedroom and waited for Liddy to put her to bed. She brought Elise into the room and helped her into her nightdress, then tucked her into bed.

"I want to tell Papa goodnight."

"He's in the library, working on something important. You'll see him at breakfast."

"What are we having for breakfast? Bacon?"

"I don't know, little one. You don't like bacon."

"Gorham does. He wants bacon for breakfast."

Liddy sighed. "I don't think Mrs. Burns cooks to suit Gorham."

"All right. Will it rain tomorrow?"

"Oh! So many questions! Be a good girl and go to sleep."

"Good night, Liddy."

"Good night, Elise." She took the lamp with her and closed the door. After only a few minutes, I heard stirring from the bed and the sound of a match striking. By pressing my eye to the crack between the two halves of the closet door, I could see Elise lighting a candle.

She spoke then, a soft whisper. "Gorham? Come out now. We can play." She moved out of my line of sight, and I heard a snuffling growl and some thudding footfalls.

Then I heard Gorham's voice. "Food?"

"I have some bread."

67

"Give." Then I heard the unmistakable sound of chewing.

"What do you want to play, Gorham?"

A rumbling growl. "Dolls?"

Elise giggled and I saw her move across the room to pick up two of her porcelain dolls. She looked at the other side of the room, holding the dolls before her. "Do you want to play with Alice or Junebug?"

I could clearly see her face when Gorham answered. "Bug."

Elise's lips never moved. Furthermore, the voice came from across the room. "Bug, Bug, Bug."

My insides felt like I'd just swallowed a pound of ice. Something was in that room with my daughter!

Elise stepped forward and disappeared from my view again. "No, Gorham, that's Junebug's hat, not yours!" She giggled.

"Hat. My hat."

I threw the closet doors open and stepped into the room. I saw Elise staring at me, her mouth a surprised circle. Beside her, on the floor, sat a two foot tall terror! It had a small body topped with a large, broad head. It's maw bristled with long pointed teeth, more teeth than I could count! It's eyes were wide with surprise and it had a doll's hat perched on its pate.

It leapt to its feet, jumped to catch the latch on the bedroom door and dashed down the darkened hall. I stood stock still, scarcely believing what I'd seen.

"Papa! You scared him!" Elise's voice carried a distinct note of disapproval.

I knelt beside her. "Elise! Did it hurt you? Are you bitten?"

She frowned. "He doesn't bite. Why did you scare him away?"

I heard breaking glass and raised voices from below. I turned to Elise. "Stay here, don't leave this room!"

I hurried down the back stairs and stepped into the kitchen. Ryman was helping Liddy up from the floor. "It was awful, sir, just awful!"

"I saw it, Liddy. Where did it go?"

She pointed through the open door. "Through there!"

"Liddy, stay with Elise. Ryman, find Campbell, Lewis and Giles, have them meet me by the stables. I strode to the library and unlocked the gun cabinet. I loaded all four pistols and both rifles. I carried the firearms outside and distributed them to the others.

Ryman stuck his pistol in his belt and looked grim. "Giles saw it, sir."

I turned to the boy, who looked to be a split-second from total panic. "Where did it go, lad?"

He pointed through the gate. "Out there, sir, on the moor."

I nodded. "Saddle the horses. Campbell, we'll need torches."

"Yes, sir. What are we hunting, sir?"

"A... I don't know what to call it. A goblin?"

Campbell shot me a frown. "A what?"

"Look, you'll know it when you see it. It's short, has a mouthful of teeth, and was in my daughter's bedroom!"

Ryman cinched the saddle on his horse. "Gorham?"

"Yes, I should have listened to you, old friend."

We rode through the gate and over the moor toward the mire. We spread ourselves out thin and moved slowly, thoroughly. I was about to give up the search when Giles called out that he had seen it, and we were off again.

69

Twice more the lad saw it running through the bracken and reed near the edge of the bog.

Ryman pulled up next to me. "Odd, sir, don't you think?"

"Odd?"

"Yes, sir, odd that it's the boy who keeps seeing the beast. Only the boy, if you see what I mean, sir."

I called the men together; we sat facing each other on horseback. "We're not getting anywhere."

Giles spoke up, in his cracking voice. "I'm sure I saw it, sir, off that way."

"Did you, lad? Show me the beastie's footprints. The ground is soft here, surely there must be footprints where you saw it running." Campbell's voice bordered on fury.

I shot a stern glance at Giles. "What are you doing, boy? Are you hoping to curry my favor by pretending to see the goblin?"

He opened his mouth as if to speak, but caught Campbell's scowl. He hung his head. "I'm sorry, sir. Very sorry indeed. It wasn't my idea, really, sir, it wasn't."

I shook my head in disbelief. "Well, just whose idea was it? Gorham's?"

"No, sir. It was my aunt's idea. She told me to lead you out onto the moor."

"Liddy? Why would Liddy . . ." My eyes opened wide. "Did your aunt kill the chickens? Did she set the fires?"

The boy sat silently for a moment before nodding once.

"Why?" Ryman gave Giles a jerk that nearly pulled him out of the saddle. "What does she intend to do?"

"She said the girl is tainted by evil, and that's why the goblin came. She said that evil only brings more evil into the world."

Ryman shook him again. "What is your aunt going to do?"

Giles wept then. "She says the girl must be purified."

"Purified? How?"

"With fire."

I closed my eyes and took one deep breath, just one, which was enough to keep me from falling apart. "Back to the house! Now!"

We rode fast and hard across the moor. Each time my mount's hooves touched the ground my panic rose, tightening my chest and squeezing the breath out of me. As we approached the house I saw something that nearly ended me right there.

Fire.

The stables and the chicken house had been set aflame and each roared as they burned. I yanked on the reins and leapt from my horse. "Elise!" I started toward the burning stables, intending to walk directly into the fire. "Elise!"

Ryman nearly tackled me. "No! Sir Warren! Don't go in there!"

I struggled to disentangle myself from him. "She could be in there!"

"No! Look! There, in the garden!"

I spun around and saw a bonfire had been built in the center of the garden. The rosebushes wilted in the ruddy firelight, and in front of the flames I saw Liddy. Only this was not the prim, correct, woman that I had known. Not at all. Her hair hung free and danced in the wind. She

71

wore a white robe of some sort and held a long, wicked silver blade to Elise's throat.

She hissed at us as we approached. "Stay back, all of you. You cannot stop what must happen here."

Lewis took aim with his rifle. "I have a shot, sir."

"No! You could hit Elise! All of you, put your guns down!" I dropped my own pistol. "Don't hurt her, Liddy."

She scowled, a madness I had never seen on her face before. "Don't you understand, Sir Warren? I'm doing this for you! You're being plagued by evil! I've seen it, watched it grow in your house! You don't know what I'll do, what I've done, to protect you!"

I held my hands out before me. "Liddy, that's my daughter you have. I love her. I beg you, don't hurt her."

Liddy shook her head. "She is a' tainted, Sir Warren, as was her mother! I saw that evil in your wife, and I ended it."

"What?" I felt my heart give a lurch. "What are you saying?"

"I saved you from your wife's evil—I saved your soul!"

Ryman took a step forward and jabbed a finger at her. "You murdered Lady Elizabeth!"

Liddy bared her teeth. "She wasn't a woman anymore! She was a devil! A devil just like this one!" She gave Elise a shake. My daughter's eyes pleaded for help. My help. "I've seen her familiar spirit, a foul beast if ever there was one."

Still holding my hands before me I took a step closer to the fire. "I've seen the goblin, Liddy. Do what you will to it, but leave Elise alone. She's all I have left."

A tear trickled down Liddy's face. "I'm sorry, sir, but I must purify the girl. By silver and fire!"

"No!"

She raised the silver blade above her head and held it there, glistening redly in the firelight. She brought her arm down, but as she did, Gorham leapt out of the hedge and sank his needlelike teeth into Liddy's forearm. She screamed and dropped the knife into the fire. Elise tore herself free from Liddy and dashed across the lawn and into my arms!

Gorham rent at Liddy with his teeth and the hard little nails on his hands and feet, and she pounded at him with her free hand. Blood ran down her face and neck, her white robe turning crimson. She stepped too close to the fire and her robe and hair burst into flame. She shrieked, a horrible sound, and fell into the fire which swallowed her and her tiny attacker whole.

"Gorham!" Elise started toward the conflagration, but I caught her and held her close to me. We wept together. "He was my friend. My only friend. Now I'm all alone."

"No, Elise, you're not alone. You'll never be alone."

She looked at me and tears ran down her cheeks. She clung tightly to my neck as she wept. I patted her back. "You'll never be alone Elise, never."

The fire burned hot, and defied our efforts to extinguish it. Later, we sifted through the ashes and found Liddy's bones for burial, but of Gorham we found nothing. His existence could not be proven empirically, but neither could he be said not to exist since he undoubtedly saved my daughter's life. Myths and magic, which I'd labeled as nonsense, can no longer be said to be untrue, and scientific tenets, which comprised my conception of the world, have toppled to the ground.

I'd heard of epiphanies, of course, but I never expected to experience one. Gorham, a creature of myth, a fantasy held by the uneducated, exists in defiance of logic and rational explanation. But reasonable or not, fantastical or not, Gorham restored my daughter to me, and for that I shall be eternally grateful. Yet now I wonder, what else exists, out there, beyond the walls of reason?

Rupert, ASP
By C. K. Deatherage

Kathleen O'Callahan wearily plopped down on the iron bench outside Mui's Splendid Dragon Take-Out. She stretched her tired legs and wiggled her feet; Mui's famous teriyaki chicken over stir-fried rice sat boxed and bagged beside her. It was a long walk back to Peterson's Law Office. There she would dine on a lonely supper while keying in the brief Mr. Peterson needed for tomorrow morning's court session. He had forgotten it until twenty minutes before the end of the work day and had asked if she could stay after to remedy the situation. She, of course, had agreed. She sighed and waggled her tired feet once more. Sometimes it was a pain being a nice person—literally.

For some reason, she had craved Chinese food tonight, halfway across town—not that halfway across the small town of Heavensent was that far—but she had decided a brisk walk would be good after a day of primarily sitting behind a desk. So, she had left her blue Ford sedan parked in front of Peterson's Law Office and half jogged the nine zig-zagging blocks to Mui's on Main Street. Having then stood in line for twenty more min-

75

utes, her feet were now protesting her excursion. That and the letter she had tucked away in her purse caused another sigh to breathe past her lips.

She glanced up at the golden dragon hovering above the restaurant. Yellow bulbs outlined its sinuous body, half of which were dark, making the "Splendid Dragon" look rather bedraggled and melancholy. Rather like herself—golden dreams of attending law school fading into the burnt-out bulbs of impossibility. Heindleman's Law School had accepted her submissions application, but there were no assistantships available. Without an assistantship, she would not be able to fund even the first year of studies using her small savings. The letter of acceptance from Heindleman's mocked her—offering the opportunity of a dream without the means of achieving it.

She blinked tears quickly, swallowing the rising lump in her throat. It would not do to let passersby see her crying in front of Mui's. She sniffed, picked up her purse and sack of Chinese take-out, and prepared for the long return trip to Peterson's.

"Hence loathéd Melancholy
Of Cerberus and blackest Midnight born
In Stygian cave forlorn
'Mongst horrid shapes,
and shrieks, and sights unholy!"

Kathleen paused as the verses from Milton's *L'Allegro* echoed down the street. Besides Miss Brunswick—the highschool English teacher—and herself, Kathleen doubted if anyone in the entire town of Heavensent knew Milton by heart. The voice drew closer as the verses continued.

"Find out some uncouth cell
Where brooding Darkness spreads
his jealous wings and the night . . ."

The voice and its owner stopped, standing beside Kathleen—an elderly man in faded brown trousers, a thin cotton shirt, and a floppy fisherman's cap of an indiscriminate grayish-brownish-greenish color. His pale blue eyes danced beneath wildly bushy white eyebrows, and equally wild bushy white hair curled around the edges of his cap. He smiled and bowed slightly, motioning towards the iron bench upon which Kathleen perched.

"May I join you, young lady?"

Kathleen blinked, then nodded and scooted over. "Actually, I was just leaving—"she began.

"Ah, what a shame," the elderly gentleman sighed. "I had hoped for a little pleasant conversation while I rested. But I reckon that's the way of it for you young folk, always on the go. Can't be helped I suppose."

Kathleen hesitated. Her mother worked at Still Waters Nursing Home just outside Heavensent, and she often went with her to visit the residents on weekends. She knew how a friendly smile and a listening ear could brighten an elderly person's day. She glanced at her watch then sat back against the bench. "I suppose I don't have to rush off right away," she said, mustering up the semblance of a smile. She held out her hand. "I'm Kathleen O'Callahan."The man's eyes fairly twinkled as he took her hand in his large calloused one and gave it a quick squeeze. "Rupert," he said with a nod. He reached inside his shirt pocket and pulled out a card, handing it to her. *Rupert, ASP*, glittered in faded gold lettering on a slightly smudged white background.

77

"ASP? What does that stand for?" Kathleen queried and absently pocketed the card.

"Angelic Sidewalk Patrol," he answered, smiling. "I'm an angel."

"I—see." Kathleen studied the man carefully. "What exactly do you do as an angel, Mr. . . .

"Oh just Rupert, please. All my friends call me Rupert." He leaned against the iron back of the bench, took off his fisherman's cap, and wiped his forehead. "Well, we of the ASP are assigned to assist people in need."

Something clicked in Kathleen's memory. Her mother had mentioned a new community group forming at Still Waters to keep the residents busy and purposeful. This Angelic Sidewalk Patrol must be it—an appropriate name for a town dubbed Heavensent.

"I see, Rupert." Kathleen smiled. "Well, I suppose even angels need to take a break." She nodded toward Mui's. "They have excellent vegetable egg rolls if you need some carbohydrates."

"Thank you for that helpful bit of information, my dear. I shall store it away for future reference. However," Rupert winked, "I'm not on break. I'm actually on active duty. I saw a rather doleful young lady in need of cheering up and thought I might offer my assistance."

Kathleen gave a lopsided grin and shook her head. "I looked that *doleful*, did I? And here I thought I was so clever at hiding my emotions."

"Ah, but you can't hide your heart from an angel," Rupert said, smiling back. He sobered. "I don't suppose it has anything to with a response from Heindleman's Law School, would it, Miss O'Callahan?"

Kathleen blinked then sputtered, "How did . . . where . . . Oh, *mother!*" She shook her head. Her mother, Maureen, a full-blooded Irish immigrant, was a lively, talkative woman who found it hard to keep secrets. She'd probably shared with the entire nursing home about Kathleen's application to Heindleman's, and now everyone in Heavensent would learn about her dashed dreams.

Rupert patted her hand lightly. "There now. I've not done such a good job at cheering you, have I, Miss O'Callahan? But I just want you to know that things have a way of working out, no matter how grim or bleak they may appear for the moment. Don't discount the workings of Providence."

Kathleen avoided Rupert's eyes as she answered, "I do believe in Providence, Rupert, but I think He might have more important things on His mind than whether or not a woman from a three-stoplight town goes to law school. Somehow I think He expects us to do our part."

"Indeed?" Rupert smiled and tried smoothing out the wrinkles in his fisherman's cap to no avail. Quirking his lips ruefully, he gave up and plopped the cap back on top of his curly white hair. "And just *why* don't you think He is immensely concerned about the future career of a lovely young woman from a three-stoplight town?"

Kathleen looked down at her fingers clenched in her lap. She forced them to relax and took a deep, cleansing breath. "I have my reasons," she answered.

Rupert sighed with her. "Yes—yes you do. I believe your father died when you were only eleven, and, though your mother, that dear woman, has worked heart and soul ever since, money has been a little tight—not much to spare for law school. Yes, I can quite see your point."

79

Once again Kathleen felt her mouth gape at the older man's knowledge of her. Just how much of their private lives had her mother shared with the nursing home residents? This conversation was beginning to get uncomfortable. She shifted, reaching for her sack of take-out, but paused and asked, "Well, Rupert, since you seem to know quite a bit about me, could you answer me this— *why* has God allowed such dark times in my family's lives? With all that's occurred, why shouldn't I doubt God cares about what happens to me?"

Kathleen cringed at her own questions, glancing about to see if anyone else had overheard. She had never voiced her innermost doubts to anyone, not even her mother, and now she was blabbing them out loud on Main Street to an elderly man she had just met!

"*Why* is a long dark tunnel with no light at the end," Rupert mused, leaning back and closing his brilliant blue eyes. Kathleen raised one eyebrow at the old man's response. He sounded like a Chinese fortune cookie. What on earth did he mean? Then he opened his eyes and gazed straight into Kathleen's. "But then, God does some of His most beautiful work in the dark," he said softly.

Kathleen drew a shaky breath and shook her head. "And just what beautiful work has He done for my mother or me?"

Rupert smiled. "Why, my dear, Miss O'Callahan, He made *you*. A gentle, sensitive soul, who, knowing what it's like to suffer and do without, wishes to change the world for the better." He leaned back and tapped his chin thoughtfully with one finger. "Yes, I think you will make an excellent lawyer."

Kathleen shook her head. She did not know quite what to make of Rupert, ASP, and his statements. It was disconcerting how he seemed to draw her deepest thoughts out.

At that moment, an explosion shook the ground, vibrating through the iron bench and sending shockwaves through the air. Kathleen leaped to her feet, eyes wide. "What was *that*?" she gasped as patrons emptied out of the restaurant and stood gaping at an orange glow lighting up the dusk of the sky off to the west of town. Soon the town's three fire trucks—sirens screeching, horns blaring—made their way down Main Street, speeding through the three stop lights, to disappear towards the mysterious calamity. The Sheriff's car and the county ambulance followed soon after.

"That's in the direction of Peterson's!" Kathleen exclaimed.

"Probably that old potato factory," a man declared as the crowd mulled about on the sidewalk.

"There are a lot of old houses out that way," an older woman murmured. Kathleen didn't comment on the fact that Heavensent was entirely built of old houses. She didn't think any new construction had happened in town since the 1950s—unless one counted the Ice Cream Shoppe on the corner of Straight and Broadway.

"Looks bad. Hope they get it contained. Might have to call in help from Northgate," the male voice said.

Kathleen felt her body moving, starting forward towards the glow. "Don't forget these, my dear." Rupert thrust her purse and sack of Chinese take-out into her hands. "And remember, only Providence can take the darkest circumstances and work them about for good. Goodbye, Miss O'Callahan." Kathleen nodded, her vision still focused to the west and the distant sirens. Several others began walking in the same direction, and soon Kathleen found herself in a large group all heading towards the old potato factory.

With the jostling and ever-growing crowd, it took Kathleen a full twenty minutes to reach the site of the fire. What she saw took her breath away. The old potato factory was indeed in flames. It looked as if half the building had suffered an air raid. Bricks and glass littered the streets, sidewalks, and yards for blocks. She had noticed several broken windows in the houses closest to the factory, but it was the Westside Business Plaza that caught her attention. A two-story brick building—nearly as old as the potato factory—housed Betty's Beauty Salon, Quick-n-Easy Roto-Rooter, Greener Pastures Realty, and Peterson's Law Offices. Located just across the narrow alley that separated it from the old potato factory, the Westside Business Plaza had shared in its neighbor's demise. The rear half of the building had collapsed, and the entire structure was engulfed in flames.

She edged her way through the crowd to the front to experience the full impact. Not only was Heavensent's entire fire department present, but three more departments from neighboring communities had sent their trucks to help contain the blaze. Then she saw it—her car, what was left of it. The windows had blown out, the blue paint singed black, three of the four tires flat. Her heart sank. Apparently, she was out of a job, a car, and a future practicing law. Tears welled. Where was Rupert and Providence now?

She stood for an uncountable period of time, watching the fire gut the buildings, the firemen doing all they could to keep it from spreading. As the blaze began to burn down, the wind shifted blowing dark smoke toward the onlookers. They quickly dispersed, Kathleen trudging slowly the seven blocks to her home, her mind and emotions numb. As she opened the front door, stepping directly into the living room, she was startled to see her employer sitting on the couch, wiping his eyes and nose with a handkerchief while patting her mother's hand as she sat next to him sobbing.

She blinked then cleared her voice. "Mom? Mr. Peterson?"

Maureen jumped up, wringing her hands for a moment. "Kathleen, child—you're alive!" she whispered as if disbelieving her eyes. Then she flung her arms open and engulfed Kathleen crying, "Lord love us—your alive!" Her mother continued to murmur into her shoulder praising God and making vague comments on some sort of miracle of the fact she had just walked through the door still breathing. She stood there trying to take it all in. Finally, she pushed back and demanded, "Yes, I'm quite alive, thank you. Why shouldn't I be?"

Maureen took her daughter's hands in her work-worn ones. "Why, darlin', you were supposed to be working late at the office. And then the gas main blew—and your car parked right there out front all black and burnt. Mr. Peterson saw it soon after the first fire trucks arrived. What were we supposed to think? Where were you, love?"

Kathleen felt a little breathless despite the fact she was standing perfectly still. "Oh my. . ." she murmured. "I'm so sorry. I should have called. I didn't even think . . ."

83

"But where were you? How did you escape?" Mr. Peterson stood watching her intently, his eyes still bright from unshed tears.

Kathleen took a deep breath and sat down in the chair by the door, setting her purse and bag of Chinese take-out on the floor next to her. "I-I went to Mui's to pick up some supper. I decide to walk and get some fresh air. Just as I was about to return to the office, an elderly gentleman from Still Waters stopped by and we started talking. We must have talked for awhile, and then as I was about to walk back to the law firm, we heard an explosion." She paused and looked up at Maureen standing near her. "Mom, I think your friend saved my life. If he hadn't come and conversed with me, I might have made it back to Peterson's just when the explosion occurred!"

Maureen furrowed her brow. "What did you say the gentleman's name was?"

"Rupert. You know—quotes Milton. Tall. Beautiful curly white hair. Fisherman's cap. Here, he gave me his card." She dug the smudged card out of her jacket pocket and handed it to her mother. Maureen studied it and shook her head.

"What does *ASP* stand for?" she asked.

Kathleen shrugged. "It means Angelic Sidewalk Patrol. Isn't that the new community group you told me they were starting at Still Waters?"

"No, child. They formed a bridge club and there's no gentleman by the name of Rupert at the home."

Kathleen felt her heart beat faster. "But—he knew so much about me—my application to Heindleman's and—and even about Dad! How did . . . if you didn't tell . . . I mean . . ." Her voice faded away.

Maureen breathed, looking up past the ceiling as if she could seen Heaven itself. "Lord be praised!" she gasped. Then she turned her sparkling gaze back upon Kathleen and placed Rupert's card in Kathleen's trembling hands. "Have you not thought that perhaps your elderly gentleman in the fisherman's cap was indeed one of the heavenly hosts? He saved your life—you said so yourself."

Kathleen had difficultly reconciling an old man in a wrinkled fisherman's cap with her vision of winged heavenly beings. And yet, how did he know those things about her if her mother hadn't told him? And what of his talk about Providence and making something beautiful out of tragedy? Could it be true? Was Rupert a *real* angel? She took a deep breath, slightly dizzy, and felt thankful she was sitting down.

Kathleen slumped in her chair, her mother crouching beside her, stroking her back. For a moment neither spoke. Mr. Peterson cleared his voice. She glanced up and sucked in her breath. "Mr. Peterson, I'm so sorry about the law firm."

Peterson brushed back his silvery-gray hair and stuffed his handkerchief in his pocket. He looked like his cheerful yet poised self again. "Well, perhaps it's for the best. I'm getting old, forgetful of things like last-minute briefs." He paused, his voice growing shaky. "My forgetfulness nearly killed you, Kathleen. If you had been there, doing what I had asked . . ."

Kathleen hastened to interrupt. "Mr. Peterson, it wasn't your fault a gas main exploded. Please don't feel badly on my account."

He smiled and took a deep breath. "I've got a nice retirement saved up, and I think perhaps I ought to, well, actually retire. You know I've been talking about it for the past three years."

Kathleen nodded, but her heart sank. That meant she was definitely out of a job. And Mr. Peterson was the only lawyer within a five-town radius. What would people do without him?

Peterson looked down at his hands for a moment as if gauging their usefulness. Then he studied Kathleen. "I understand you are planning to go to law school?" he asked.

"I've applied to Heindleman's and they've accepted, but I need to find a way to pay for it," she answered honestly.

"Yes, well . . ." Peterson cleared his throat. "I've been thinking about that, and I'd like to fund your way, if you'll let me."

"Saints be praised!" Maureen exclaimed. Then turning to Kathleen, she added, "I told you the good Lord would provide a way."

Kathleen abruptly stood. "Mr. Peterson, that is very generous, but I don't want you to feel obligated because of what happened tonight."

Peterson shook his head. "I can think of no better person I'd rather have to replace me," he said. He held up his hand and added, "And that is the one condition I place upon the transaction. The first six years of your practice must be here in Heavensent and to the surrounding communities. After that, if you wish to move on, you may do so. Could you agree to that?"

Kathleen smiled, tears again welling in her eyes. She held out her hand, which Mr. Peterson grasped in his. "I'd like nothing more," she whispered.

Mr. Peterson nodded. "I'll leave you now. You've got quite a bit to think about tonight." He patted Maureen on one shoulder and let himself out.

Her mother shook her head. "My goodness! Angels and explosions and now this! The good Lord surely works in mysterious ways." She paused, bent down and picked up Kathleen's sack of Chinese take-out. "There now—you've eaten naught a bite since lunch, I fear, and this is stone cold. Let me warm it up for you."

As she turned toward the kitchen, a small object fell from the sack. Kathleen bent to pick it up—a fortune cookie. She sat back down in the chair by the door, mechanically unwrapping the cookie, while her mother hummed in the kitchen. Breaking the cookie in two, she popped one half in her mouth and unrolled the tiny slip of paper tucked inside the other half. She read it, paused, and read it again. Then she began to laugh until she cried. Her mother came in, wiping her hands on her apron. "Why, darlin', what's gotten into you? Should I call the doctor?"

Kathleen shook her head and handed Maureen her fortune. Her mother scanned the few words printed beneath the suggested lottery number and smiled. "There you go, child. There you go," she said. Then she turned and went back to the kitchen. Kathleen read the fortune one last time before popping it into her pocket next to Rupert's card:

You have friends in high places.

87

The Gift
by C. K. Deatherage

The rain cascaded in a steady waterfall off the edge of the back porch roof, the sky gray and flat, mirroring the mood of the man huddled against the stone wall of the funeral home. Jonathan tugged on the collar of his black suit-coat, having left his overcoat in the building, and tried to put a little more warmth between himself and the chilly, damp weather. He sighed. He knew he should return to the mourners inside, ready to paste on that sad smile and acknowledge the condolences of family, friends, and acquaintances over his brother's death, but just twenty minutes into the visitation time he felt he needed a breather. Not that it was easy to breathe in the moisture-laden air. His soul felt as heavy as the rain-filled clouds above. Unbidden, he felt a tear mingle with the wet air on his face. It surprised him—he thought he was all cried out.

Just two days ago, he and David had been joking in his living room after their two families had shared a supper. Two days ago, David had declared plans to take his family on a vacation to Florida to visit all the touristy attractions. He had wanted to make a lasting memory for his three kids—Michael, 10, Jamie, 8, and Jonathan, 3. Well, they'd have a lasting memory alright—just not the one David had hoped for. A drunk driver had seen to that.

Jonathan clenched his fist. It wasn't fair! The drunk didn't have a scratch on him—but David had been broadsided and killed instantly. He gazed up into the roiling clouds and shook his head angrily. What had God been thinking? Why take David and a leave worthless drunk to roam the planet? What possible good could come from leaving Jessica without a husband and the kids without their father? "Why?" he whispered into the drizzling grayness. Only the sound of a steady down-pour answered back. He shook his head and began to turn, when a movement caught his eye. He paused. A dark form began to emerge from the blank gray of the rain—a man wearing a tan overcoat and a black Fedora. He walked slowly, coming up the steps of the porch to stand beside Jonathan.

The two men faced each other, studying each other. Jonathan noticed the stranger was Latino, short black hair glistening with raindrops where the Fedora failed to protect it, dark brown eyes bright with intensity. The man nodded. Jonathan nodded back. "Your prayer has been heard," the man said in a strong yet quiet voice, slightly accented.

Jonathan blinked. "I beg your pardon?"

The Latino spoke again. "Your prayer has been heard. You asked *why* your brother was taken. You feel it is unfair, that God made a mistake."

Jonathan shook his head. He could not deny what the stranger said, yet how could the man know his inward thoughts? It was too unsettling. He edged closer to the

89

door to re-enter the building and escape the strangeness of the situation. The man reached out one gloved hand and placed it on his arm. Jonathan froze—literally. He couldn't move. His heart began to pound. What was going on?

The Latino took off his Fedora with his other hand and smiled. "Do not be afraid. God has sent me to give you a special gift, a gift that will answer your questions and more." Jonathan felt a warmth spread through the arm the man was holding. A pleasant tingling traveled from his shoulder to his right hand. "This gift will allow you to heal—even to restore from death itself. It may be used only once. You will also be given a glimpse of Divine insight to guide you in your decision."

Jonathan found his voice. "Who are you?" he whispered.

The man replaced his Fedora and removed his hand from Jonathan's arm. He gave Jonathan one last smile. "You may call me Angelo," he said and then he stepped out into the rain, his form merging with the downpour, fading into the grayness.

Jonathan flexed his right arm. The warm tingling remained. He glanced up at the clouds. If it were true, if God *had* given him some sort of gift, a special power to heal, even to resurrect the dead, there would be no need for Divine insight. He knew what he would do. He turned and strode resolutely into the funeral home. Coming from the back entrance, he managed to avoid most of the well-wishers as he made his way to the chapel and entered through a side door. Jessica and the two older children stood near the front and to the right of the coffin along with Jonathan's parents and own wife, Belinda.

The coffin was open to allow viewers to see David's face one last time and make their farewells.

Jonathan nodded to Belinda, who looked relieved to see him return. He smiled and shook several hands as he made his way to the coffin. There, he gazed down upon his brother's face—paleness artificially colored with mortuary make-up. The mortician was good at his work, but it was still plain that David's soul, his life-force, was gone. All that remained was an empty husk. Jonathan felt the tingling increase as he raised his right hand and placed it on the coffin. Dare he touch David's face with others looking on? Was there some prayer or command he should give to release the power he felt surging in his arm? He hesitated, and at that moment his vision went black.

In the blackness, lights began to appear, each one linked as if on a huge web. The web with its lighted nodes spread out into the inky darkness as far as he could see, and yet, instinctively, he knew it went on infinitely. He felt himself drawn to one of the shining lights. Peering into its illumination, Jonathan saw Jessica. She was older and looked tired but content. She wore a nurse's uniform, and Jonathan remembered that Jessica had been a nurse before Michael was born. Michael was there too, preparing to go to college. Somehow Jonathan knew he would become a counselor. That was strange. Jonathan thought Michael had wanted to learn computer programming to design games.

He followed a thin strand of light to another node where he watched an older Michael counsel a troubled young man. The young man, in turn, became a police officer, responsible for saving the lives of an entire family as he assisted the firefighters who fought the flames that consumed the family's home. One of those family members was a baby, three months old. Following another strand, Jonathan saw that infant, grown, and practicing medicine in a clinic somewhere in Haiti, saving even more lives. Jonathan blinked. What was going on? Why was he seeing all of this?

Jonathan's vision shifted to another node and saw his niece Jamie, now a young woman, wearing a life guard vest, a whistle hung about her neck. She was working over the summer to earn money for college—as money, without David's income, was tight. She noticed a young girl struggling in the deep end of the pool, blew her whistle and plunged in. She reached the girl, just as the youngster was sinking beneath the chlorinated water, and pulled her to safety. Another strand, another node, and the young girl was now a microbiologist working for the CDC. She had discovered the inner workings of a certain malarial strand which resulted in the formation of a viable vaccination, saving countless lives in malaria-plagued countries. One of those saved by the vaccination was a young African man, who eventually became a strong leader in his country and, for a time, brought peace and prosperity to his people. Jonathan began to shake. If David were alive, he would have funded Jamie's college education without her having to work summers. If David were alive, that little girl whom Jamie saved might have drowned. Without that little girl becoming a microbiologist . . .

Jonathan laid his forehead against his right hand, still tingling, still waiting for him to use his gift. He didn't want to see any more. He wanted to touch David's body and see blood coursing beneath that pale skin, see those blue eyes open, hear David's bright laughter as he bounded out of the coffin to join his astounded and joyful wife and children—children who would make different choices with different outcomes, choices that would affect the lives of possibly thousands. A sob caught in Jonathan's throat.

Another node, another vision. This time he saw a short man with sandy-blond hair. He was standing in a courtroom being sentenced to probation and instructed to enter an alcohol treatment program or risk jail time. This was the drunk driver whose car had struck and killed David. The man began well, but his guilt over David's death and his alcoholic cravings caused him to binge after only three weeks of treatment. This time he twisted his old Buick around a tree, leaving his own family without husband or father. Life was hard. The mother worked as a check-out clerk at a local grocery store. One teenaged son overdosed. Another joined a gang and ended up in prison for assault with a deadly weapon. Jonathan knew this vision represented what would happen to the drunk's family if he did *not* raise David from the dead. Catch-22.

A noise from the back of the chapel broke the vision with its infinite web of nodes. Jonathan blinked and looked up. He turned to see what was causing murmurs to flow through the crowd of mourners. A man had entered, followed by his wife and two small sons. He wore a shabby gray suit, his tie crooked, his sandy-blond hair falling into one eye. The man looked scared, uncertain. He hung against the back wall, arms protectively around his sons who leaned against him while staring out at the crowded chapel. His wife, too, entwined her arm through one of his. They looked like a small band of frightened sheep. Jonathan drew a shaky breath. Tears blinded him for a moment. "I'm sorry," he murmured. The words took in David and Jessica and their three children. They covered his grieving parents, his wife, and himself. And somehow Jonathan knew they echoed into that inky, web-filled darkness.

He wiped his eyes and stepped away from the coffin. He caught Jessica's glance as she smiled quietly and nodded. He strode to the back of the chapel to where the small family stood huddled. He held out his hand to the sandy-haired man. "I'm Jonathan, David's brother. Thank you for coming."

"I—" the man slowly raised his hand. "I'm sorry. I'm so sorry for all of this. Please tell her"—he looked in Jessica's direction—"how sorry I am."

Their hands met. Jonathan's arm buzzed with heat. The man stood straighter, less intimidated, a new light in his eyes. Jonathan smiled. "She knows," he said quietly.

The man took a deep breath. "I haven't had a drink since that day—and I never will. I promise."

"I believe you." Jonathan released the man's hand. His arm no longer tingled. "It took a lot of courage to come here today," he continued. "I appreciate your thoughtfulness."

The man coughed. "Yes, well, we don't want to disturb things, so we won't stay. I just wanted you to know. And the kids here, they have a card for the family." One small boy stepped forward and held out a smudged envelope. Jonathan took it.

"Thank you," he said.

As the man began to usher his family out the door, he locked eyes with Jonathan, and Jonathan noted the determination, the strength of will in that glance. He knew the gift was already at work. Then through the doorway, he caught a glimpse of a tan overcoat and a black Fedora. Angelo was leaning against a light post across the street. Their eyes met. The Latino touched his hat with his fingers, then turned and followed the sandy-haired man and his family as they disappeared into the rain. Jonathan flexed his hand and took a deep breath. It would be a hard road for Jessica, for the kids, for all of them, but in the end, it would work out. He gazed into the downpour and smiled. Yes, it would work out—for *everyone*.

Poetic Oddities

The Ghost of Cap'n Crow
by Larry D. Rudder

A tall and rugged figure leaned up against the door
of Robby's Blowfish Tavern on Brierburton's shore.
His visage, rough and haggard, made all men step aside
to enter Robby's tavern and for a time abide.

When they all were settled, a story-teller stood,
lifted up his brew and said, "Aye, ye know 'tis good.
Ye've dropped in to lift yer mugs and toast yer final day.
So set yerselves, drink it up, and hear what I've to say.

"So press around, ye maties, and hear me gruesome tale
of a pirate and a fisherman et up by a whale.
Cap'n Crow was the pirate; the fisherman no one knows.
But heed me well to what I say—and listen mighty close!

"Yon whale, he weren't so choosy about his daily meal.
He swallered hisself a main mast and et hisself a wheel.
But 'ol Crow, he were a helmsman and the wheel it
    were quite stout,
so he fixed her to the whale's tail to steer it 'round about.

"The fisherman was a hefty man and heaved the sail, no
    doubt,
and hurled it to the foredeck, then rammed it up the spout.
And in the storm, the waves heaped up—the wind was
    fearsome strong.
Yet Crow stood firm upon the deck and whistled a lusty
    song.

"The ocean wind named Eurus, she blew a fortnight long,
in echo to the whistle Cap'n Crow blew loud and strong.
The men, they holds their courses in waves that heave
    and roil,
and Eurus laughed aloud to watch the sailors at their toil.

"She then caught up the canvas and set the sail avast—
the Cap'n and the fisherman was headed home at last.
The whale stuck hard upon a reef and bellered out a
    roar.
Out blew men and main mast and landed on the shore.

"Ol' Crow leaped up and grabbed the mast not knowin'
    what he done;
The other grinned a toothy grin and thought 'twas all in
    fun.
But Crow, he conked the fisherman and stole his gold
    and all,
grabbed up all the loot he took and went to have a ball.

"He laughed and sung the song he thought he heard ol'
    Eurus sing,
but Eurus tossed a mighty wave and gave the man a fling.
She drowned the Cap'n in the sea—made sure that he

was dead.
But still there's them that say they hear ol' Crow
    a'singin' yet.

"Strange, it is, to hear the truth o' such a wondrous tale,
But if ye doubt just what I've said, then lift yer mugs o'
    ale,
And look ye 'round at yonder door—the figger that ye see,
'tis ol' Cap'n Crow hisself, as bold as he can be!"

The crowd turned 'round to see who stood—a tall and
    swarthy man.
They swallowed spit and backbone, then each one
    turned and ran.
The back door splintered at their rush to flee the
    stranger's gaze—
those squinted eyes that seemed to burn with Satan's
    fiery blaze.

The figure shoved his way right through the swinging
    tavern door,
started toward the bar but tripped and stumbled to the
    floor.
"Git off yer face," the spokesman said, "and git ye to
    the stool
before they all come back and see yer just a drunken
    fool!"

The man stood up a'boilin' mad and tossed a fearsome
    frown.
Without a blink, he drew his sword and cut the fellow
    down.

"I don't mind them," in wrath he growled, "what calls
    me to a duel,
But no man dares to call ol' *Cap'n Crow* a drunken fool!"

The Devil's Holiday
by Larry D. Rudder

'Twas a sad affair at O'Leary's Lair
when the devil came out to play.
He danced and he pranced and he nearly entranced
all the folks what lived on the bay.

Ol' Nick played a trick with a magical stick
when he broke up O'Patrick's ball.
Everyone knew he put frogs in the stew,
and then he started a brawl.

The king became bitter and sent for the critter,
hoping to bring to an end
all the evil and fuss that could make people cuss
and soon realize that they had sinned.

The king's men they found him smokin' a pipe stem,
and grabbed him and tossed him around.
The troops was defeated and thus they retreated—
the devil was off with a bound!

He then sailed to Wales to give her some ails,
and sailed back to O'Leary's lair,
where he thus settled down to make sinners in town,
and cause witchees to fly in the air.

Now I know what you think, 'cause I see by your wink,
that you doubt that my story is true.
But I have this to say, and may all rue the day
that I uttered these words—Fie on you!

Ol' Jigger
by Larry D. Rudder

There once was a dog that got lost in a fog.
He weren't really much of a hound.
'Cuz he dropped to his knees and started to sneeze
From the dirt and the dust on the ground.

Each sneeze brought a howl 'cuz the ground smelled
    so foul;
the sad cries echoed loud through the land.
The dogs all around joined the mutt's woeful sound,
and in chorus they raised quite a sand.

The lights in the town on the streets up and down
only showed up a bit in the fog;
and it made the poor cur make more of a stir,
'til he croaked all the more like a frog.

Every door opened wide as the folks poured outside,
just to see what was causing the noise.
"Sounds like Jigger next door. He's done this before,"
came the shout out from one of the boys.

"Poor old pooch doesn't know where he's lyin' so low.
Hope he don't die from yellin' so hard."
Soon the fog disappeared; it was just as they feared:
The old dog was laid out in his yard.

If you think it's a sight when a dog dies of fright,
you don't know that much about Jigger.
'Cuz late every night when the fog kills the light,
you can still hear him howlin' with vigor.

Strange Places
by C. K. Deatherage

Slim Jim—a mirthful name
for one so wide of girth.
See, Cowboy Slim, bull-rider of fame,
was chubby from his birth.

But that's not all the mystery
puts awe upon our faces.
'Cause Slim made rodeo history
by landing in strange places.

One bull flung him far afield.
He landed all kersplat!
His face so scratched, it bled and peeled—
he'd landed on a cat!

That cat let out a horrid yowl
and laid in with a vengeance.
T'weren't places left on cheek or jowl
That weren't bereft of skin, gents!

C. K. Deatherage

Another time, with arms amuck,
his midriff all a bouncin',
he landed on a flatbed truck,
and—laws!—he took a trouncin'!

The truck there held a roll of wire
all bright with gleaming burrs.
Ol' Slim he yelled as if on fire
when he felt those silver spurs.

Oft times within the bar he'd ride
the ale-house bucking bull,
and once it flung him far and wide
into a table full.

Now listen, folks, that table had
six cowboys wild and tight.
They plied poor Slim with whiskey bad—
he nearly died that night!

Many a time a bull had thrown
Slim Jim into strange places.
His last ride out, his body prone—
he landed where his face is!

Old Slim's retired these past twelve years;
he walks with cane and braces.
It comes from years of bulls and beers—
and landing in strange places!

Dust—A Lament
by C.K. Deatherage

Dust is my enemy,
  Dust is my doom.
Dust dims my daylight,
  Dust fills my gloom.

Dust on each bookshelf,
  Dust coats each book.
Dust on my knick-knacks,
  Dust in each nook.

Dust 'neath the bedstand
  reached with a broom.
Dust in each corner,
  Dust in each room.

Dust in the sunbeam
  through window pane.
Dust where I dusted—
  I dust once again!

C. K. Deatherage

Dust in my garden
  blown by the wind.
Dust ground in kids' clothes—
  never an end!

First as a youngster,
  now fully grown,
Dust fills my daily chores.
  Dust I bemoan.

Next in the graveyard,
  down in the loam,
Dust in my coffin
  lies by my bones.

Dust when I'm living,
  Dust when I'm dead.
Only Hereafter,
  no dust will I dread!

The Peasaunte and the Knighte
By C. K. Deatherage

Windeth sond of battail hornes,
sword on sword and thruste of spere,
byrnies ringing warding blowes—
falleth he and dyeth there.

Falleth dead, unseen, unfoughte,
his bodye lieth, battaile-bounde
Warriors gaineth, warriors loseth—
sweat and blood pour'd on the grounde.

But I sawe him stumble, struggle,
pushing thro the knightly throng.
Scarce a beard upon his faytures—
one forsaykin, loste and yong.

Garments homespun, shoes well-worn,
naught but club bare he in hond.
I nevere sawe him strike, nay none.
He only soughte for safer lond.

But nevere lefte he from that feld.
Upon his hed a blade dyde falle.
Upon the grounde, his bodye laye,
his eyes upon brighte Heven's Hall.

I pitye him, this peasaunte lad,
who from his home was taken then
to fighte a battaile not his own—
he shall not retourn to kin.

The mightie lord takes up his men,
and from the feld they travell on.
He careth naughte for peasaunte lad,
or those who weep and mourne ther son.

Een those who theeve the dying, ded,
turn from the peasaunte's muddyed frame.
He holds no gold or silver fayre.
The beggars, too, pass him in shame.

I spur mine mount on thro the press,
but halte besyde the peasaunte youth.
And fain would I dismount and stay,
but I ryde on to war and rooth.

The Knight and the Peasant Youth
By C. K. Deatherage

Amidst the war-filled sounds of horns and battle cries,
the clang of sword on sword and thunk of spear on shield,
the jangled ring of chainmail warding off a blow—
amidst this orchestra of death he falls and dies.

No one sees him fall, nor do they seem to care.
The battle rages on. One side and then the other
gaining ground, then losing, gaining back again,
inches bought with blood and bodies—none to spare.

But I, I saw him stumble, struggle, try to steer
his young frame through the thronging mass of clashing
    knights—
and young he was, scarce having grown his first rough
    beard,
his blond hair falling in his eyes grown wide with fear.

His clothes were but brown homespun wool, his shoes
    well-worn.
He carried in his hand a simple wooden club—

113

I never saw him use it once on man or beast.
He merely sought to leave this field of bitter harm.

He never left. A flashing weapon scored his head.
He fell there then upon the trampled, bloodied field,
his brown clothes melding with the churned up mud.
His blue eyes gazed unseeing heavenward—yet dead.

I pity him, this peasant taken from his home
to fight a battle not of his own wish or will.
I wonder who his parents are and if they'll learn
he'll not be coming back but lies bereft, alone.

The war-cries fade, the victor gathers up his men
and leaves the field with jingling of his fancy arms.
I wonder if the peasant boy was his; if so
the mighty lord cares nothing for the dead—or him.

The thieves who raid the wounded, dying, and the dead,
ignore the young man's muddied, bloodied frame. They
    know
just by his simple clothes he holds no gold or silver.
Even beggars pass him by upon his bed.

I spur my weary horse on through the battle's press
and pause beside the body of the peasant youth
and for one moment I am tempted to dismount,
but I ride on to fight again—while *he* will rest.

Creature Comforts

A Rock and a Hard Place
by Larry D. Rudder

Around, gray rock, about the size of a coconut, rested on top of an embankment about two inches from the edge of the crusty surface. It was a smooth, almost polished, rock with two round holes, barely two inches apart, seemingly drilled into its surface.

There were no hills, no other terrain, above the bluff that could have deposited the rock at that spot. It was as if it had been placed there by design, or else had somehow moved to its precarious position by its own volition.

A hot gust of wind puffed across the land gathering small clouds of dust and sand, tossing the debris over the edge of the hill. The particles cascaded briefly into the precipice before dispersing into the air, seeming to disintegrate into nothingness.

The rock quivered under the force of the wind, moving gradually closer to the edge with each gust, until one final push caused it to drop the distance to the sloping side of the hill. The circular stone fell like a cannonball, and the movement of air across the two holes elicited a whistle that almost sounded like a child's scream that

117

was hushed when the rock struck the sloping part of the hillside. The missile tumbled rapidly toward the tiny rivulet, slowed when it reached the soft cushion of sand in the creek bed, and stopped short of the water.

The two holes faced the top of the bluff as though they were gazing at the sun that was now disappearing behind the rim. The air turned cold, and a trace of dew began to gather on the rock, causing its surface to glisten when a full moon appeared above the horizon.

Days passed—hot days and cold nights—with no movement except for an occasional bird flying overhead, or a lizard hopping up on the rock to gain a better vantage point from which it could survey the terrain, only to be struck by a snake that had been resting against the opposite side of the rock, then to be swallowed—still squirming for its life—until it became nothing more than a lifeless lump in the serpent's belly.

Another day passed, and a gray wolf lifted its leg against the rock, marking its territory, and leaving a scent that protected the rock from further violation—except for the high-pitched buzzing of a few flies and a mud dauber that interrupted the silence of the hot afternoon. Steam radiated from the rock, casting rippling shadows on the sand.

A loud crack rang out, and a crease appeared in the rock beneath the two holes—creating what looked like a twisted grin on a round face. The cracking sound was accompanied by a sudden sharp squeal that ended when a small piece of lead buried itself beside the rock.

Finding a convenient place to build its nest, the mud dauber began to fill one of the holes with clay. The damp material quickly hardened under the unrelenting heat of the sun's harsh rays. After several days of constant activity, the tiny wasp ventured away and never returned—perhaps becoming another victim of its environment.

As the darkness of night enshrouded the creek bed, the wind whipped up swirls of dust, and a fox raised its nose to smell the odor of rain in the air. The animal cocked its head to one side as though it had heard a noise in the distance and moved nervously away from the rippling water.

The noise that had at first only been noticed by the fox slowly grew from a slight rumbling sound to an almost deafening roar. The ground shuddered, and the tiny stream began to move more rapidly, growing in size as the noise increased, until a frightening wall of water plummeted down the small valley that stretched along the bluff.

The rushing current lifted the rock and shoved it into the middle of the coursing stream, smashing it into the rough sides of the winding creek bed, and jarring the mud dauber's nest free from its encasement. The two holes and the twisted crease took on the appearance of a terrified grimace as bright lightening flashes filled the sky and exposed the features of the rock.

The rock rolled up on the bank of the stream as it reached a sudden turn in the channel and came to rest beneath another overhang of the bluff. The deluge beat against the rock until the wind finally died down and the rain ceased.

The next day presented a cloudless sky and a hot sun that brought steam from the rock's surface once again. The raging stream slowly dissipated and returned to its former strangled condition, and the rock was alone—

Larry D. Rudder

alone in the silence of a timeless, almost barren land—a rock with two holes that stared upward, its twisted crack a hesitant grin—a solitary rock that awaited another lizard, another wolf, and another storm.

The Beast
by C. K. Deatherage

The beast was huge. Even my mother was dwarfed by it. It walked on its hind legs and used its front paws to catch things. It caught me, scooping me up and holding me tightly to its chest. I froze where it placed me. I'd never been this high from the ground before. I decided not to look down. I looked up instead and studied the beast's head and face. It looked odd, fur covering only the top and back portions of the head while the face seemed bare. The fur on the rest of its body was strange too, shifting and moving under my feet. The beast gazed down at me with round eyes and bared its teeth. I shrank back. Yet, its stare did not seem threatening. And it began a gentle, high-pitched crooning, which seemed at odds with its bulk and size. It reached out one paw and began to stroke my head and back, as if to coax me to relax, to trust it.

But how could I trust something so humongous and strange? I glanced down at my mother who pattered around the beast's hind feet, keeping one eye on me and the other on my siblings, whom the beast seemed to ignore. Yet, despite my anxiety, I felt my body relax under the constant stroking and its soft murmurs. That's when the beast made its move.

Slowly, it turned and strode away from my mother, away from my siblings, away from the only home I'd ever known and carried me to a terrifying creature, which sat hunched on its four feet, hairless and shiny in the sun. The beast touched the shiny creature's mouth and it opened wide. Then to my horror, the beast stepped inside the creature's mouth and sat down. We were going to be eaten! I clung desperately to the beast's chest, waiting for the crush and crunch of savage teeth. The creature in whose belly we now sat roared then growled and started to move. I hid my face in the beast's fur as the creature grumbled and vibrated around us. It seemed to go on forever, but then, as suddenly as it began, the creature stopped its growling and was still. The beast shifted as the creature's mouth opened once again and spat us out. I peeked over the beast's shoulder as we walked away from the terrifying creature, amazed we had come through uneaten. The creature sat as it had before, on its four feet, hunched over, naked and shiny in the sun.

I turned my attention to where we were going. It looked like a huge square hill with a funny angular top. The beast, still holding me to its chest, walked up the hill and into a cave opening. Inside the hill were tunnels and more caves, punctuated here and there with holes where the sun came in. The beast took me to one of the side caves and slowly knelt on its rear knees. I dug my nails into the beast's fur as it tried to lower me to the ground, but the beast gently pulled me free and set me down.

I stood there for a moment, not knowing what to do, where to go. Then my curiosity got the better of me. I love to explore, and there were so many new things to see in this cave. I wandered around, poking here and there at odd things made of wood and others made of something shiny like the creature in whose belly we rode. In one corner I found a box with dirt in it—or something like dirt. It was more gritty than the garden where I was used to walking. I glanced back at the beast who remained crouched, watching me. I needed to relieve myself and this seemed the most likely place to do so. I did what my body required then hurried to bury it, so as not to draw attention to my presence. Not that the beast was unaware. It made a pleased noise when I had finished with my toiletries.

The beast rose, bent down and picked me up again, placing me by a strange container that held delicious-smelling food and sweet water. I tasted the food—it was different from what my mother gave me, but it was good! I ate until my belly was full, then took a long drink. By this time, after all my adventures, I was tired. But where could I sleep that was safe? At home, I had my mother to watch over me and my siblings to sleep with, but here in this cave with a strange beast watching me, where could I sleep?

I decided the beast itself was the best source of safety. It was certainly big enough to protect me from other creatures. It even tamed the shiny monster that had tried to eat us outside the cave. I walked over to it and called to be held. It seemed to understand, for it scooped me up in its huge paws and held me close to its chest again, making that soothing crooning sound. As it stroked my head and back, I felt myself relaxing into its clasp. Somehow I knew that my life was going to be very different

123

than what I had experienced with my mother and family. Yet, life with this curious beast might prove interesting. It seemed to care for me—I could feel its affection in its paws and hear it in its soft murmurs. I curled up, contented, on its chest, listening to the murmur of the beast's heartbeat–and began to purr.

As Long as There's Chocolate
by C. K. Deatherage

My folks got Chocolate 'fore I was born, so I can't 'member him as a puppy. For as long as I've known our chocolate Lab, he's always been a big ol' gangly dog with floppy ears. His tail wags so hard it could chop a saplin' down, and his breath is so bad it could kill a skunk. He's old now and don't do too much but follow us around when we're outside or beg for table scraps when we're inside. Oh yeah, he can shake hands and play dead. 'Course he don't always get up when I tell him to after playin' dead. He just lies there and thumps his tail like he's tryin' to whack a hole in our floor, which kinda ruins the idea of playin' dead.

I wish I could tell you of some great adventures we had growin' up together, me and Chocolate. You know, like the ones Old Yeller had savin' people from wild boars and mad wolves and going huntin' and stuff like that, but we live on a small farm not too far from town and there ain't any wild boars or wolves. The closest thing we got to wild animals is Sally Mae, our sow, who'll charge you if she's got piglets. Chocolate's smart enough to stay away from her, though if he could bark a body to death, she'd be a goner fifty times over.

I once tried to write a school essay on how Chocolate saved our lives by barking up a storm and pulling the sheets offa us as our house filled with smoke when our chimney blew up. But Mom made me throw it away 'cause our chimney never really blew up and our house never filled with smoke. Mom said that essays are supposed to be true stories, and mine warn't. I thought that was a dumb rule—still think it is—but you can't argue with moms and win.

So instead of writin' boring ol' essays that have to tell the truth, I started writin' made-up stories about me and Chocolate. (Mom said it's okay to tell made-up things in stories 'cause they're "fiction," which, I guess, are lies that are okay to tell and won't make you go to the Down Place, unlike if you tell whoppers in a school essay.) I think I got about twenty of 'em, stories, I mean. My favorite is where me and Chocolate travel back in time and meet Robin Hood. We join his Merry Men (and one dog) and beat the tar outta the evil Sheriff of Nottingham and his soldiers. Chocolate even bites a hole outta the trousers of the Sheriff!

'Course Chocolate never really bit nobody, though he barks his head off when folks come to our house. He 'specially likes to bark and snarl and drool whenever the egg man comes to buy some of Mom's eggs. If he's outside, he'll pace around the egg man, at least ten feet away, and sound ferocious, but he won't get any closer. So the egg man don't even bother to look twice at ol' Chocolate.

I'd kinda like to see Chocolate bite Billy Barkley down the road. Billy's real mean and teases a lot of us kids. Once he pushed me down when I was hikin' home from school, and I scraped my knee. I wished Chocolate had been with me, but even if he had, he's got so many teeth missin' that I don't think he coulda done much harm even if he *had* bit Billy. Maybe he coulda panted in Billy's face and made him sick to his stomach.

You might wonder what's the use of a dog like Chocolate? I mean, he can't hunt, he don't bite, he's never saved our lives, he's too old for most fun stuff like sneakin' up on my cousin Jennifer when she comes for a visit and scarin' her. He mostly just lies around, thumps his tail, and grins a happy, stinky, mostly toothless grin when you pat his head. But for all that, I think I would miss him if he was to play dead for real. So would our cat.

Now *there's* a story. I nearly forgot—Chocolate *did* do something brave once. He saved our cat—even before she was our cat. (Actually, we got lots of cats, but most are wild and live in the barn, unlike our cat who lives in the house.) She was just a kitten at the time. The night was awful, a real thunderstorm with rain and hail and lots of thunder and lightnin' filling the sky. Chocolate was doin' his usual "I hate thunderstorms!" thing of hidin' behind the couch, when all of a sudden he sprang out and bounded to the back door, whining as if he needed to do you-know-what.

"You don't really want to go out there, do you?" Mom said as she got up to let him out.

He just whined some more, so she shrugged and opened the door. The wind whipped in along with a lot of rain, but Chocolate bolted out as if the thunder-storm were inside and safety were out. Mom stood there watchin', letting the rain soak her skirt. I saw her eyes grow big and she waved my Dad to come to the door. He put down his book and hurried to see what had her all excited.

"Well, would you look at that!" he said.

In popped Chocolate with a tiny wet kitten clutched in his jaws. She was covered in mud up to her neck and mewin' louder than some of the thundercracks, which was somethin' for a critter so small!

"Oh, the poor thing!" said my sister Meg, who al-ways cries whenever Mom kills a chicken for Sunday dinner. She started to tear up now, but Mom put a stop to it.

"Now, don't go to fussin'. It looks like Chocolate heard her mewin', probably from the ditch out back, and went and rescued her." (How Mom knew it was a *her*, I don't know, but it was.) "Let's go clean her up." So Mom and Meg went to wash down the tiny kitten while Dad gave me the job of towelin' off Chocolate and wipin' his feet with the rag we kept near the door for just that pur-pose. 'Course, Chocolate just *had* to shake hisself and threw half the mud of the ditch off onto the walls, the chair, and me 'fore I was done. So I ended up takin' a bath too.

Once the kitten was cleaned up, we could see she had a golden yellow color. I said we should name her somethin' that goes with "chocolate," so we named her Butterscotch Puddin', but we just call her "Puddin'" for short. It's weird, but Puddin' somehow knew Chocolate saved her. She'd cuddle up to Chocolate's stomach and purr loudly any time Chocolate was in the house, and Chocolate would lie there lickin' Puddin's face and back as if she was a pup he was sittin'. He never barked at Puddin', though he loved to bark at most of the barn cats, who just ignored him. And Puddin' never hissed or spat at Chocolate. They were and are the best of friends. Sometimes we still find them sleepin' curled up together, and they *both* head for the back of the couch in a thunderstorm.

Yeah, I bet Puddin' would miss Chocolate if he was to, you know, *pass on.* But he's gettin' old. His joints creak—I can actually hear them crack when he heaves himself up. And he's goin' blind and is a little hard of hearing. Mom looks at him, pats his head, and clucks her tongue. "It's only a matter of time," she says sadly. I sometimes wonder what life would be like without that bag of boney fur lying all splayed on the floor, tail thumping, gums grinning in hopes of some scraps or a good head scratch. Who would I have to write stories about? It just ain't the same with Puddin'. What could Puddin' do against the Sheriff of Nottingham but scratch his ankles? I just can't think up any good stories about a cat and me having adventures, though I like Puddin' almost as much as I like Chocolate. It's just not the same. There's somethin' about a boy and his dog—even an old stinky-breath one like mine. So, I've promised myself to keep writin' stories about me and Chocolate.

'Course this isn't a story. This is an essay since I haven't told any "fiction," 'cept the parts about me and Chocolate and Robin Hood, which ain't the same as just telling you a story.

129

I wrote this for school and when Mom read it ('cept for the part I'm writin' now), she got all teary-eyed and said I did a good job. I hope, Miss Cranston, you think so too. If you do and I pass my class, I can say Chocolate saved the day again, just like he did with Puddin' and like he always does in my stories. There's always a happy ending as long as there's Chocolate.

The Gray Dimension

Going Home
by Larry D. Rudder

The day had begun with a brilliant sunrise and an icy glaze that coated everything in sight. The frozen crystals on the barren tree limbs sparkled with the reflected rays of the sun, and icicles hung like transparent stalactites from the overhanging rock formations that lined the hills on each side of the wooded glen. The temperature remained below zero throughout the day. It was a dry freeze.

In the evening, a light powdery snow began to fall, covering the ice with a thin white blanket that continued to build until a heavy crust formed over the ground. Then the wind picked up—strong gusts that blew the snow into deep drifts along the hillside. By nightfall a full-scale blizzard developed. The snow was no longer powdery but fell in large, heavy flakes that flattened against the drifts, driven hard by the wind.

A lone figure moved through the trees, staggering against the wind and snow with an obvious determination to overcome the forces that had been unleashed against him. Bill Branson fought his way along a narrow path that had once been a logging road but now was

133

barely discernable. He was convinced that the storm was created by a supernatural power and designed to keep him from reaching his destination. He shouted a plea for mercy toward heaven then swivelled his head toward his dark surroundings and cursed the unseen enemy that moved among the trees.

Bill knew he had been followed when he escaped the old brick building that had been his prison for so many months, and he knew he had to keep moving to avoid being caught. That had happened before, but he swore it wouldn't happen again. Not this time! He would never go back alive—back to the dingy corridors that smelled of urine and echoed with the moans and screams of others who were being held against their will–people like himself who had done nothing to warrant imprisonment.

This time, though, he had located a rifle in an unsecured storeroom, and he was determined that no one would stop him from getting home. Home was a place of safety. His wife and children were there, and his mother and father, who had a room in the rear of the cabin, would be there to help. Even in their advanced years, they would fight to the death to protect their son.

Bill closed his eyes against the bitter wind and pictured Melinda standing in the open doorway of the cabin, framed by the glow of lanterns and the flickering flame of the fireplace that would be ablaze with a roaring fire— little Becky with her arms around her mother's legs, anticipating her daddy's homecoming. He could see his teenaged son, Tim, beside Melinda, holding the shotgun he had given him for his sixteenth birthday. Tim would be ready for a fight when Bill's pursuers caught up with him.

Gotta get home, he thought. *They need me as much as I need them.*

Bill shivered, his teeth chattering uncontrollably, as the icy gale rushed through tears in his flimsy jacket— the only thing he could find to wrap himself in as he fled through the door at the back of the building. The cook had failed to pull the door tightly closed when he had taken the garbage out that night, and Bill had seen his chance to escape. He was sure he would make it. He had never gotten this far before.

"They'll play hob gettin' me this time," he muttered. "I gotta good start on 'em." He gave a quivering laugh. "'Sides, they don't know about this loggin' road. Time they find it, I'll be home."

He wanted to find shelter from the cold, but he knew he dare not stop for anything. His pursuers might not be as far away as he hoped. They could catch up at any time. *Gotta keep movin'*, he thought. *Gotta get home.*

There was a sudden snap above his head, and Bill spun around and looked up. A large snow-laden tree limb, bowed beneath the weight of winter's frigid blast, cracked like a rifle shot and dropped. Bill couldn't move fast enough and soon found himself engulfed by a mass of tangled branches—escaping the main limb by a few short steps.

He lay still for a moment, wondering if he had been impaled by any of the twigs or had broken any bones. He had suffered some scratches and a couple of deeper cuts, but there was no pain. Perhaps the severe cold kept him from feeling anything. It even seemed to stifle the flow of blood.

135

Slowly Bill pushed his way out from under the web of branches and stood to his feet. His legs were weak, and he waited to see if he would be able to walk. He looked at the pile of limbs. "Maybe it'll work to my good," he mumbled. "It'll slow them devils down a little." He groped in the snow for his rifle. *There it is*! He pulled the gray barrel from beneath the branches.

Once again the half-frozen man plodded forward, more slowly now, using the rifle as a crutch—at last feeling soreness in his legs and arms. *That's good*, he thought. *Shows I got life in 'em. Not froze yet.*

It seemed as though he had waded through the snow forever—snow that was falling in heavy waves, almost like a dense fog. Bill rubbed his eyes and for the first time realized that he had lost his gloves. A strange light brought his attention to his hands—hands that now had developed a blueness to them, with white patches forming at the ends of his fingers. *Ain't sore no more. O Lord! Please not yet! Let me get home!*

He fell forward into a hard ice-covered object—a wagon–blocking the path, and a sudden noise came from behind him. "They caught up!" he cried. Raising the rifle, he tried to pull the trigger, but his frozen finger couldn't find it. "You ain't takin' me back! You ain't!" He pointed the rifle, hoping to frighten them off.

Then he turned his head and peered around the large wagon that had stopped him. "I made it!" He could see Melinda just as clearly as he'd imagined. There she was standing in the doorway of the cabin with little Becky. "Melinda! Melinda! It's me! I'm home!"

"Papa? Is that you?" a voice from behind him called.

"Tim? Timmy? Are you there, Timmy?"

"Yes, Papa. It's me."

"Thank God I couldn't find the trigger. I'da killed you for sure!"

A small crowd gathered around his nearly frozen figure. Bill tried to force his white lips into a smile. "That you Mama . . . Daddy? I made it, didn't I? I'm home to stay! Who's that with you?"

"These men have come to help, Papa. Don't worry—we'll get you back."

Bill sank down into the snow, took a deep breath and slowly exhaled, closing his eyes, his lips still holding a smile as Melinda and his folks welcomed him into the brightly-lit home.

One of the men knelt down over the limp body. "He's dead." He reached down and pried the cane from Bill's hand—which had continued pointing at them as if it were a weapon.

"Looks like he got caught in that pile of old lumber when it fell over behind the shed back up the alley. Worked him over pretty good too," the attending officer said. "I can't believe he made it this far in the cold—wearing nothing but his pajamas like that. He must've used every back alley in town to keep from being spotted before he bumped into that dumpster."

Tim wiped his eyes and studied the smile on his father's lips. "Well, he won't fight it anymore. Walked away from the nursing home three times, but this is the end of it."

Becky had been standing under a streetlight at the end of the alley, and she hurried over to where her dad lay against the dumpster. "He escaped for good this time, didn't he?" she said. Her eyes glistened with tears that weren't quite ready to fall.

Tim reached out to touch her cheek. "He was always talking about going home to be with Mama and Grandpa and Grandma. I guess he's with them now."

They gazed down at Bill's frozen smile. "You're right," Becky whispered. "He made it home after all.

Tessie
by Larry D. Rudder

Tessie sat in the corner of Cornelia's bedroom with her face toward the older lady who perched on the edge of the bed attempting to knit a pair of miniature shoes—Cornelia's hobby from her earliest years. Time had taken its toll on the gray-haired woman. Her arthritic fingers could no longer manipulate the needles, and she muttered words of frustration. Cornelia sighed and glanced at the petite figure in the small rocking chair.

"We're such good friends, aren't we, Tessie? And you're such a good girl!" the eighty-three year old woman said. But Tessie remained silent, and Cornelia continued to speak. "I don't know what I'd do without you to keep me company. That boy of mine ain't worth a dime when it comes to visiting with me. Link promised to come over today and change the light bulb in the kitchen. You heard him. He knows I can't reach it. Now look here, it's almost time for *Gangbusters*, and he ain't here yet."

Cornelia put her needles in the basket that she kept beside her bed and painfully edged herself off the mattress into a standing position. The arthritis in her knees made walking such a chore that she usually spent her time either on the bed or on a firm straight-backed chair by her radio.

As she passed the window, she stopped long enough to draw the curtain back and look out at the street. "He's here, Tessie, and he brought that wife of his along. I wish he'd leave her at home. She gripes my fanny. All she does is criticize and nag. You know she does. We gotta do something about that woman!"

She watched as Link pushed open the door and heard him call out, "We're here, Mom! Just keep your seat. No need to get up on our account." Link entered her bedroom, his wife following closely behind.

Cornelia glared at her son. "You get a job yet? My money ain't going to last forever, you know." Her daughter-in-law's mouth curled at one corner. "What's your problem?" Cornelia asked, noticing the smirk.

"Your money will outlast *you*," the woman responded.

"Now, Deb," Link broke in, "we don't need quarrels. Let's just do what we came to do. Come on in the kitchen with me."

Cornelia sat back down on the edge of her bed. "See what I mean, Tessie? She just plain gripes my fanny. There's no two ways about it!" She could hear the couple's voices through the open wrought-iron register between the two rooms.

"Just take a whiff of that!" Cornelia could hear Deb's coarse whisper. "She hasn't changed the litter box in weeks. It's a wonder the cat doesn't keel over from the stink!"

Link chuckled sarcastically and pointed at a dark pile under the table. "The cat doesn't use it anymore. But what do you expect? Mom can't bend down to take care of it. She can't even use her fingers, what with her arthritis."

"Well, *I'm* not cleaning the nasty thing, so don't even think about it. Your mom belongs in a nursing home. You know she does."

Link's voice tightened. "And if we put her away, do you still think she'll help us with our bills? You know she's our grubstake. Besides, if you expect me to inherit those bonds of hers, we'd best take care of her now."

"She doesn't need that money, Link, and we need it now. What'll we do if we lose our house? Those bonds are worth forty-five thousand dollars! We need to see a lawyer and have her declared mentally incompetent!" Deb was no longer careful to keep her voice down.

"Shush! You want her to hear us?"

"Look around you," Deb went on. "The house is filthy. The stove is so greasy it's a fire hazard, and all she does is sit in her bedroom talking to herself. Just listen!"

Cornelia was in the process of whispering to Tessie. She lowered her voice even more. "They ain't gonna put me away! We'll just see about that. All they want are those bonds Jacob left me. Well, it'll be a cold day in hell when they see one red cent. They already drained my bank account—even got what was in my purse. Just see if they get any more."

The two in the kitchen strained to make out the whispered words. "See what I mean?" Deb growled through her teeth. "It won't be hard to prove she's lost her marbles."

141

Deb moved to the doorway to listen more intently to her mother-in-law's whispers, while Link stood on the kitchen table to replace the bulb in the ceiling fixture. Climbing down, he gripped his wife's arm, pulling her away from the bedroom door. "Come on," he said. "Let's go." Then he called to his mother, "Mom? We're leaving. We'll let ourselves out. Just stay where you are." He pulled Deb to the front door and quickly shut it behind them.

Cornelia lifted Tessie to her bosom and leaned against her pillow. She could no longer hold back the tears. "Ungrateful! That's what they are! To think I used to wipe his butt and nurse him at the breast. It's that woman! She's turned him against me, that's what. Makes me sorry I ever brought my boy into the world."

She sat up and reached for the glass of water she kept on the night table by her bed and painfully fumbled for some aspirins that were in a small bowl beside the glass. "Tessie, which of these pills is my aspirin? I can't tell them apart without my glasses." She fingered the pills in the bowl. "I think these are them." She pulled out a few white pills and swallowed them, then leaned back again.

The next evening, Link and Deb returned to tell Cornelia of their plans to put her in the nursing home. When they stepped inside the door, the odor almost overwhelmed them. "I'm going to burn the trash," Link muttered. "Maybe that'll get rid of some of the stink in the house."

"Not likely," Deb growled. "It's that cat litter."

Link stared at the corner by the sink. "No," he said, pointing. "Look there. It's the cat. Been dead no telling how long. That must've been some of what we've been smelling." He pinched his nose.

"Well I'm not picking it up," Deb said.

Link shrugged. "I'll take it out with the trash." He grabbed the sack that rested inside the door, pushed the cat in with his foot, and carried it out to the back yard. He tossed the sack on the ground on what Cornelia called her "burning spot" and set fire to it.

"Link, you'd better get in here!" Deb yelled from the bedroom window.

Link hurried to Cornelia's room. His mother was lying on the bed, holding a tattered old rag doll under her chin. The button eyes had been gone for years, but Cornelia had placed her glasses where the eyes should have been. The doll's dress was torn and dirty. The only new material in the old doll was the thread that had evidently been used to repair a ruptured seam.

"Mom, are you okay?" Link shook his mother's shoulder. Cornelia didn't stir. He blinked then swallowed. "I think she's dead, Deb."

Deb didn't seem to be listening. "Just look at her! She's dug that stinking old doll out again!"

"She's dead! Didn't you hear me?" Link glared angrily at this wife.

Deb jerked the doll from Cornelia's lifeless body and stormed out of the room. She scurried out the back door—straight to the fire Link had started. With a snarl, she threw the doll into the flames. "Stupid old woman!" she nearly screamed.

Link stood at the door and watched his wife's senseless actions. "What in the world are you doing?" he demanded.

"I didn't tell her to die! It's not my fault!" she shot back.

"Well, get in here so we can decide what to do," he said.

The next day, they went to the bank to open Cornelia's safe deposit box. Link had found the key in the top drawer of his mother's dresser. He was uneasy about opening the box so soon. "What will people think?" he muttered to his wife. "They'll say we're just after Mom's money."

"Who cares what people think. We have a right to those bonds," Deb answered in disgust. She frowned at her husband. "Let's just get it all and go."

Link opened the box and found a folded piece of tablet paper. Written on the page were the words: *I gave the bonds to Tessie. I told her to take care of them.*

"Tessie? Just who is Tessie?" Deb groaned. "She's let somebody we don't even know take those bonds, Link! Those were bearer bonds. Anyone can cash them! What are we gonna do?"

Link bowed his head, his voice a hollow whisper. "Forget the bonds, Deb. We'll never see them. Tessie was her doll." He glared at his wife. "Stupid woman."

Transitions
by Larry D. Rudder

A dark, black wall of meaningless space broken by flares of colors, sometimes white, sometimes yellow or various tints of green, red, and orange, was the only vision Glen Wentworth had. *Space* because there was nothing tangible about the wall. *Wall* because there was no perceptible depth to the space.

Glen felt something beneath his back, yet he couldn't discern what kind of surface it was. Sometimes the pressure felt as though he were lying on a sheet of plywood. At other times he seemed to be floating on water. His senses were confused. His nerves didn't respond to any particular stimulus—if, indeed, any stimulus was present. And his muscles were useless, as though they were paralyzed. He tried to move but couldn't tell whether any part of his body was actually in motion. He assumed there was no response. He was hot, he thought, or perhaps cold, since he believed he was naked, covered at times with a thin piece of material—or only a breeze from an open window in that black wall.

He didn't know where he was or how he got there. He thought at times that he might be drifting somewhere

145

in space or floating far beneath the surface of an ocean. He could hear sounds—garbled sounds that seemed to be coming from a considerable distance. Perhaps echoes. Or perhaps the moans one might hear in Hell.

That's it! He thought. *I'm in Hell—or on my way there. Is this what it's like? Why not Heaven? Which is it?* These strange sensations continued for an eternity. Yes, that's what it was—but maybe not. Who could know how much time had elapsed since he had found himself in this incredible state? But then, what is time when you're floating somewhere in an endless universe of nothingness? *Am I dead—or am I just dreaming?* Dear *God, what is happening to me? Where am I? Oh God, help me*!

Something began to shift, to change unexpectedly, and Glen thought his prayers were about to be answered. He heard voices—familiar voices—and the blackness was beginning to evolve into a dim light. He thought his eyes were closed, but if so, he wasn't able to open them. But the voices were becoming quite clear. He was sure there were people standing beside him, even hovering over him.

Judy? He thought. *Is that you, Judy?* He tried to speak, but his mouth felt as though it were sealed shut. He could hear no sound coming from his throat, not even a groan.

"Is there any hope at all, Dr. Vale?" the voice said.

It is *Judy*! *My daughter is standing beside me—but I can't reach out and touch her.*

"I'm afraid not," the doctor's voice responded. "He's been in a coma for six months, and we haven't detected any sign of activity at all."

"I've been fighting this decision ever since he fell."
Judy's voice was quivering. It sounded as though she
might be crying—or at least trying to keep from it. She
continued speaking. "He always said we were not to
keep him alive by 'extraordinary methods,' but it's so
hard when you reach that point. How do you decide just
to cut off your father's only possibility to go on living?"

*That's it! I've been in a coma! Glen thought. Judy,
I'm coming out of it! I know I am. My senses are getting
sharper. I can finally feel the sheet on my body. I can't
open my eyes yet, but I can see the light through my lids.
Oh God, help me tell her!*

"Mrs. Brighton," the doctor spoke in a calm voice,
"he is, after all, seventy-eight years old. Didn't you tell
me he said he was only promised seventy?"

Glen heard Judy sniff, and when she spoke, her voice
was soft. "I guess you're right. The Lord only promised
us seventy years in the Bible, and he has had a pretty
good life—at least until Mom died. He's talked so much
about how he misses her. Maybe he's just one step closer to being with her, and my delay is keeping him from
reaching her." She paused, then said, "Would you give
me some time alone with him?"

"Certainly," Dr. Vale said. Glen heard footsteps
walking away. Then the doctor spoke once more. "It's
a tough decision, but I think you'll work it out." A door
opened then shut.

Glen felt his daughter's warm breath as she leaned
over his face and took his hand in hers. "Daddy, oh Daddy, why did you do this to me? What should I do? I don't
want you to leave me yet."

Judy, honey, I'm not leaving you. Look! I'll move my eyelids. He strained to open his eyes, or squint, or blink, but Judy gave no hint she saw anything.

"Squeeze my hand, Daddy—anything! Give me a sign that you hear me! Please!"

I am, baby. Feel that? He tried to put pressure on her hand—to move a finger. *There. Can't you feel that?*

"Is seventy-eight years long enough, Daddy? I just want you to stay with me a little longer. There are so many things I want to tell you—how much I love you, how thankful I am that I'm your daughter, for all the things you've done for me—for the way you loved Mama and me."

Glen felt a wetness on his face—Judy's tears. His chest grew warm. He wanted to cry too. *No, baby, seventy-eight years isn't long at all. It seems just a little while ago that I was holding you in my arms and tickling you under your chin. And wasn't it just the other day I bawled you out about coming home so late from that first date?*

"Daddy, I miss Mama—and I know you do too. But I don't want to miss *both* of you."

Glen wanted desperately to comfort his daughter. *I won't leave you, honey. I've got more reason to stay now. You'll see. I'm coming out of it. Just watch me.*

He felt Judy squeeze his hand. "Feel that, Daddy? Now, you do it too."

Glen tried to move his fingers again. *There,* he thought. *You can feel that, can't you?*

He felt Judy lay her head upon his chest as she sobbed. He wanted to pat her back the way he did when she had fallen off her first bicycle, but she pulled away and stood up.

"I've got to go, Daddy. I'll see you again, but don't worry. Everything will be okay." Glen could detect a strain in her voice.

There were footsteps. Glen could hear Judy speaking in the distance. He thought she was talking to Dr. Vale, but he couldn't make out the words. Tears came to his eyes and seeped through the closed lids. He could feel the moisture trickle across one of his temples.

There's your sign, Judy. Come back and take a look! He strained to listen, trying to jerk himself awake the way he had once when he'd heard Judy cry out from her crib. Another sound. There was someone in the room—someone near his bed. *Judy, is that you? Look at the tears, honey! See? I'll make it after all.*

There was no sound from his visitor, but he knew Judy was bound to lean over his face. Then she'd kiss his tear-filled eyes. Maybe that would be all he needed to open them. There was no kiss, only gentle, quiet movements. He sighed inwardly. *I'm so tired*, he thought.

He felt a pressure in his head, and the old darkness began to return, taking control of his senses. He started to relapse into that feeling of weightless space and numbness. As he drifted, he thought about his sweet wife Hannah and how much he really did miss her. Then his thoughts became broken . . . unconnected. He felt weak . . . empty . . . sounds becoming garbled, fading into silence.

Then a small light began to grow, and a voice sounded near. Glen almost thought he could feel his stiff lips break into a smile. *Hannah*, he breathed. He reached out to touch his wife, senses bursting with sight and sound and warmth. He had never felt so—*alive.*

149

The Scent of Summer
by C. K. Deatherage

The cold March rain continued its steady drizzle as Robert took a moment to gaze around the circle of his three siblings, four cousins, and their spouses. His own wife stood on his right side, one gloved hand holding up the large, black British umbrella they had bought upon arriving in London. Her other hand clasped an ornate cigar box, sealed with duct tape, to her chest. He sighed, shifting to make certain the hardbound journal he held in his left hand avoided the rain. An all-expense-paid trip to England would have been a highlight in all their lives if it weren't for the timing and the circumstances. If Uncle Jim had passed on in June, the weather would have been much nicer for a British gravesite service. As it was, the drizzle dampened their already glum spirits.

Jim had been a favorite uncle for all of them. His ready smile and fun-loving spirit that had so brightened and enlivened their childhood had held fast even to the end. He had never married, and his brother and two of his sisters had passed on years earlier. His remaining siblings were too old to make the long trip to England, so Jim's nephews, nieces, and their spouses were the only ones present at the gravesite. Robert shook his head slightly. Why Uncle Jim had wanted to be buried in a tiny cemetery outside of an obscure English village remained a mystery. Yet, it was a mystery for which, it appeared, he had prepared for a long time. He had left sufficient funds and specific directions for his burial. So, here they were, standing beside a newly dug grave, Jim's coffin already lowered in and resting in the damp earth. Robert's wife cleared her throat softly, signaling it was time to begin.

"Well, folks, we are gathered here to . . ." he paused as he watched a four-door sedan pull up near cemetery. A gray-suited driver got out, walked to the back door and opened it. He assisted the exit of a small, elderly woman with one hand, holding a large umbrella with the other. The woman steadied herself with a cane, then taking the driver by his free arm, the two made their way slowly toward the gravesite.

Robert watched with interest. Perhaps this woman had known Uncle Jim when he was stationed in England during the War. She looked old enough. As per Jim's request, they had put a notice for the gravesite service in the local obituary upon their arrival but had not really expected a large turnout from the local population—or, for that matter, *any* turnout. This was a surprise.

The woman and her driver halted some yards back, apparently not wanting to intrude. She looked up at Robert with brilliant blue eyes and gave a slight nod. Not knowing what else to do, he nodded back and proceeded with the service.

He cleared his throat. "We are gathered here to bury James Robert Sherman, retired Corporal in the U.S.

Army, a veteran of World War II, and a beloved uncle, as per his wishes. Jim left in my care his journal, sealed and bookmarked, as you can see, and this cigar box, also sealed, to be opened at his gravesite and buried with him. His letter stated he wanted me to read certain portions of his journal, written during the War as we bid him our final farewell. So, let's begin."

Robert loosened the gray duct tape that bound the old journal, wadding the sticky sealant into a ball and stuffing it in his overcoat pocket. He turned to the first yellow bookmark, placing his thumb at the next marked passage, and began to read:

June 15, 1943

Planes smell different when going out and returning from a mission, I think. Going out they smell of grease and fuel and polished metal, sometimes mixed with fresh paint as the airmen apply names and sarcastic expressions on the bombs they'll be dropping over Nazi territories: Big Bang Bertha, Berlin or Bust, and Handshake for Hitler are some of my favorites. I grin, reach over, and pat the painted beauty on the nose of the plane I am cleaning. The blonde in a white blouse, tied at her bosom, and blue shorts smiles back at me with ruby lips. Beneath her enticing form is the name Sally Mae.

"Hey, Jim!"

I look down from the ladder and see George Hancock, the gunner for Sally Mae. He is shaking his finger at me.

"Don't you go mooning over Sally Mae, now. She's our lucking mascot. Haven't lost a man or a mission yet with her gracing our crate!" George grins up at me. I grin back and wave him off with the cleaning rag I'm holding. He walks away chuckling, while I continue polishing the hull of the craft. With all the shrapnel these babies take and all the rain that falls in England, we need to keep the rust at bay. I frown as I notice an unpatched bullet hole beneath the pilot's cabin. Any higher and the pilot would have bit the dust—and maybe Sally Mae and her crew along with him. I shake my head.

I finish my work and head for command to pick up a three-day pass—the first in many weeks. I had decided to go to London. Bob Cantler had told me of this canteen not too far from Trafalgar Square. I am determined to acquaint myself with it.

June 16, 1943

I hitch a ride on an Army Air Forces Jeep heading for London. The driver drops me off at a hostel many airmen stay at when in town. After getting directions, I head for the canteen. For some reason I find this a rather heart-thumping adventure. Maybe it's because I'm a Montana country boy in the middle of a bombed-out yet bustling city. History oozes from every building. The passage of centuries palpates in the cobblestone beneath my feet. The air itself smells *old*. Yet for all the ancient-ness around me, I feel invigorated. And nervous. I'd never actually visited the London canteen before. I do not quite know what to expect.

I find the address and descend crumbling steps to the lower level of a several-storied brick building. Part of the roof had been blown off earlier in the Blitz, but the lower levels remain untouched by bombs or demolition. Pushing open the door, I find my sinuses overwhelmed by

153

smells. Beer, ale, cigarette smoke, perfume, sweat, hair spray, even the woolen scent of uniforms pummel my nose. But through all the olfactory confusion, one aroma tingles my senses—donuts! My mouth waters—as do my eyes through the fog of tobacco smoke. I don't smoke and the blue haze that hangs in the air nearly chokes me.

I make my way past dancing couples to the bar where I order a rare glass of milk and abscond with about six donuts handed to me by a smiling green-eyed USO gal. I find a seat at a table tucked in a corner and spread out my feast. As I am about to take the first bite, I hear a lilting laugh and a British voice comments, "You, sir, truly are a Dough Boy with all of those pastries!"

A perfumed musk, like the scent of roses at full bloom, fills my nostrils. I look up to see a young woman smiling at me. She wears a British Army uniform, but her auburn hair is undone. It rolls in a wave over her forehead and cascades down between her shoulders. I notice the insignia on her shoulder. It looks medical. A nurse most likely. I hastily get to my feet and motion to the chair opposite me.

"Please feel free to help me eat them," I say, feeling at once both incredibly smart and unbelievably stupid.

She puts her hand to her throat and laughs. "Oh, I couldn't deprive you of your sweets! Besides I find them much too sugary for my taste. Give me scones and jam any time."

I open my mouth to say more, but she just nods and meanders her way through the crowd to another table. Several nurses are sitting at it—but no males. I hurriedly wolf my donuts, washing them down with the milk. I stand, straighten my uniform, tuck my cap under my left arm, and maneuver my way to the ladies' table. For some reason, this nurse with her British accent, auburn tresses, blue eyes, and rosy summer-time scent fascinates me. I am determined to meet her, talk to her, get to know her.

"Excuse me, ma'am," I say, stepping up to the table. All four pairs of eyes turn to look at me, but I only take in the blue pair. "Would you like to dance?"

The young woman shakes her head and smiles. "What? You've finished your sweets already? My, you must've been hungry! But—I am here with friends. I'm sorry, soldier. I'm sure some of the dancers will accommodate you."

My face must have shown my disappointment because the other nurses at the table immediately begin to badger her.

"Oh, be a sport and give the Yank a dance!" says a brunette.

"Yes, he's come all the way across the Atlantic just to dance with the likes of you," nudges a dishwater blond.

My hopes begin to rise with the banter, and our eyes lock. She hesitates a moment, then smiles. "Why not? Very well, soldier. But I must warn you, I don't jitterbug. Slow dancing is more my style."

I swallow and return her nod. "That's just fine, ma'am. I don't jitterbug too well myself."

Amid the "Oohs!" and "That-a-girl" of her comrades, the British nurse stands and takes my arm. We glide out to the dance floor. I tuck my cap at the back of my belt and gently take her hand in mine. She places her other on my shoulder, and I feel a pleasant shiver. The crooning of a Glenn Miller tune wafts from the radio on the bar and we begin to dance. Then we dance some more. Finally, when the rhythm of Tommy Dorsey begins a faster pace, we sit down at the little table tucked in the corner. I ask a waitress if they had any tea and scones with jam. She says they do. I order some and sit back. I'm not sure where to go with the conversation, but my companion handles the situation smoothly.

"I suppose I should formally introduce myself." She holds out her hand, which I take lightly in mine. "How do you do. My name is Summer McAlister. I'm a nurse, a lieutenant [pronounced "leftenant"], in the British Army based southwest of London."

A lieutenant? I hadn't considered she might outrank me. I lick my lips. "I am Corporal James Sherman of the United States Army Air Forces based at . . . uh, south of here." I recall my "Loose Lips Sinks Ships" training not to speak of military locations in public places.

"Corporal Sherman, a pleasure to meet you. You are an excellent dancer, and I must admit to being charmed by your gentlemanly ways. Not all Yanks—that is, American soldiers—are as polite as you."

I feel my face grow hot, but I am saved from further embarrassment (pleasurable though its source) by the arrival of the tea and scones. Both smell delicious, though I usually prefer coffee. As we eat our snack, I'm desperate to keep the conversation going, but Summer saves my fumbling efforts with a simple, "So tell me about yourself. Do you have any family?"

"Have I got family!" I say, grinning. "I'm the second male of six siblings. I've got one brother, four sisters, and only one john."

"John?"

I search for the British word. "Uh, W.C."

She laughs. It sounds like her perfume smells—of summer and the frisky winds that play with the chimes my mother hangs from our back porch.

"One brother and four sisters. I always wished for a sister," she says, wiping her mouth with the red cloth napkin from the table. "I'm an only child. My father died before the War, and my mother presently lives with her sister while I'm away."

I can't imagine such a family-less situation. I pull out the letter from Janet, my twelve-year-old sister, that I had picked up just before going on leave. "With four sisters, not to mention my mom, I get letters every week. The fellas tease me for it, but they like it when I read one to them. Would you like me to read this one to you?"

"Certainly." She leans forward, blue eyes alert, her chin resting on one hand.

I clear my voice and begin reading, trying not to glance up at the picture in front of me. Janet writes about her school project which involves collecting grease from restaurants to recycle for the war. She finds it disgusting and smelly but does her patriotic duty. She relates how Sarah, my nineteen-year-old sister, laments the lack of nylon stockings as the material is being used for making parachutes. Then she goes into great detail of the trials of giving Scruffy, our large Golden Retriever, a bath. It appears he had gotten into some of the grease she had collected. Trying to wash grease out of the heavy fur of a reluctant retriever in a tin tub is nothing short of a miracle. Janet's adventures have both of us laughing until we have to use the red table napkins to wipe our eyes.

"You have a lovely family," Summer says, dabbing her eyes. "Quite charming."

157

"Yeah," I admit, "they're something alright." I think fast. "You know, I could pass on my family's doings and other news if you'd correspond with me. I'd like to get to know you better." I wait tensely as Summer re-folds her napkin. Her face reveals nothing. Then she meets my eyes and gives that terrific smile of hers.

"I'd like that."

I beg some scrap paper off of the bartender, and we exchange base addresses. I don't know how late it is, but we've danced and talked and laughed a long time. Finally, one of her nursing friends comes over to our table.

"Heigh-ho, Summer. The girls are going back to our bunks. Are you coming along or will you stay some more with your Yank?"

Summer rises, and I stand to my feet.

"I'll come." She turns to me and offers her hand. "It's been nice chatting with you, James. I look forward to hearing from you in the future."

"You bet." I give her hand a light squeeze before releasing it. I follow her out with my eyes then sit back down at the table, turning the scrap of paper with her address over in my hands. "You know I will, sister," I murmur. And I will.

August 27, 1943

I find I'm more faithful to write Summer weekly—sometimes several times a week—than I am at writing my folks. I keep my promise to pass on family news, but I also share my own experiences. She shares hers. Over the course of these past several months, our letters have grown deeper. We share what life was like before the War—and what we hope life will be after. We reveal some of our hopes, our plans, even our fears. Summer sent me a poem she wrote from the hospital:

> Youth shattered by bullets,
> aged by bombs—
> eyes grown old with war's horrors
> reflect fatigue and fright at first,
> then dim to nothing:
> a soldier dies in my arms.

That one poem does it for me. I am determined that after the War, I will take Summer to someplace safe. Someplace where young men won't die in her arms and bombs won't buzz overhead and burned out buildings don't line the landscape. I'll take her home to my family—as my wife. Through the course of our correspondence, I've discovered that Summer is four years my senior, but that doesn't matter to me. I love her, and I feel pretty sure that she has some deep affections for me. So, I will plot my next move.

September 2, 1943

When I learned of my next leave of absence, I hurriedly wrote Summer to see if she could finagle a three-day pass to London as well. Turns out she could. We plan to meet at the same canteen.

I collect my pay, hoping it'd be enough for a ring—if I can find a jeweler in London. Then I head for the city.

She is waiting at the table, our table, tucked in the corner, when I arrive. I weave my way through the dancing patrons, keeping my eyes fixed on her auburn waves. As I near, I breathe in her flowery fragrance. She smells of roses.

"Hello, Summer," I say.

She looks up and smiles. "Hello, Dough Boy."

I sit down. She looks tired. Dark circles ring her eyes and there is a slump to her shoulders.

"You alright?"

She nods, still smiling, but her eyes look guarded. I swallow, maybe this isn't a good time to propose. We eat and talk, keeping the conversation light. We dance a little. Time passes. Night falls. Still I bite my tongue though my heart burns to ask her to marry me. I offer to buy her a decent meal at a little bistro I passed a few blocks away. She agrees. We walk in the darkness, carefully picking our way over broken sidewalks. An occasional yellow sliver shines through the blackout curtains in the windows. I glance up at the stars visible between the outlines of buildings and clear my throat.

"You know, it's hard to imagine those same stars shine down on my family in Montana," I say.

She looks up at the celestial lights but doesn't respond.

I take a deep breath and plunge on. "I'd like to take you there someday, to see my folks."

Summer stands still, so do I. I can't see her face in the darkness, but I can sense her discomfort.

"Is something wrong, Summer?"

She is silent for a moment, and I can hear my heart pounding in my ears.

"I've greatly enjoyed our correspondence," she begins, and I can hear the reluctant note in her voice. "I've shared things with you that I've told no one else. But . . ." She sighs. "Perhaps, we should consider . . . maybe it's time to stop. Things are becoming . . . complicated."

160

I swallow, reaching out to touch her cheek with my fingers. "It doesn't have to be complicated," I say slowly. "I love you, Summer. I want to make you my wife."

Silence. She moves away from my touch and draws a shaky breath. "I'm very fond of you, James—"(Fond? My heart plummets)—"but marriage? . . . I'm afraid it wouldn't work. I'm sorry, James. And I'm sorry if my letters gave you the wrong impression."

I stand there silently. I don't know what to say, to feel. My emotions are a jumbled mess. My hand clenches the wad of money in my pocket, money that will never purchase a wedding ring. She touches my arm.

"Thank you for the lovely evening and for sharing with me through your letters. I shall treasure them—and our friendship—always. But now," she steps back, "I think it best we part ways. Somewhere, there's an American girl just waiting for such a fine soldier as yourself. I pray you find her. God's blessings on your life, Dough Boy." She walks away. I remain frozen, watching her shadow fade into the surrounding darkness, her rose-blossom scent lingering a moment longer. I can't even call out. My tongue refuses to move. I feel as if my heart has suffered a Blitz all of its own. I know there is no American girl waiting for me. There is only one woman I love—and she just walked out of my life. Forever.

Robert closed the journal and wiped at his eyes with his free hand. His cousin, David, cleared his throat. "Well, I guess that explains why he never married and why he wanted to be buried here. He left his heart in England."

Jenny shook her head sadly. "So many years ago, and yet he still loved his British nurse. How very sad and yet how poetically beautiful!"

Robert tried not to smile at his sister's remark. She was always a bit sentimental in her expressions. "Yes, well," Robert began, "Uncle Jim wanted us to bury his journal and these letters with him." He nodded to his wife, who carefully pulled off the duct tape and opened the cigar box. Within nestled yellowed letters, each carefully tucked inside its envelope. A faint scent wafted from the box—as of rose petals pressed and preserved between the pages of an old book.

"Roses," Jenny said, breathing in the scent as the family clustered around the box. "No wonder Uncle Jim filled his yard with rose bushes. I always thought he just enjoyed their summer fragrance, but now . . ."

Robert reached in the box and handed each one a few of the letters. He held his own handful over the open grave and let go, scattering them over the coffin. Each of his siblings and cousins did the same. "Rest in peace, Uncle Jim," he murmured. They each stood there for a moment, pondering, then, turning, they headed back to the van that had brought them to the cemetery.

Robert paused before stepping up into the vehicle. He looked back at the gravesite. The old woman had moved forward, holding a shaky hand out over the grave, and dropped a letter of her own into its depths. She looked over at him and gave another brief nod. Robert nodded back and watched as the driver in the gray uniform slowly escorted the elderly lady back to the sedan. The wind picked up, the drizzle having ceased momentarily. Robert breathed in and smiled. A faint tinge of roses wafted on the air, the scent of Summer.

Authors' Biographies

C. K. Deatherage earned her B. A. and M. A. from Southern Illinois University at Edwardsville in English and her Ph.D. from Purdue University in Old and Middle English Language and Literature. Her previous publications include *Waysmeet: Poems and Tales of Fantasy and Wonder*, "Niall MacDonaugh and the Leipreachan" in *The RudderHaven SFF Anthology I*, "Final Entry" in *Star Trek: Strange New Worlds V*, and various poems in anthologies and journals. She won the 2013 Poet of the Year and the 2013 Vardis Fisher Award for Most Humorous Piece by the Idaho Writers League. She currently resides in Idaho with her husband, two kids, two large dogs, and four cats—and an occasional very *temporary* field mouse.

Larry D. Rudder holds a B.A in history and government, M.S Ed. and an S.D. in Counselor Education. He also has a Secondary Education teacher's certificate in History, English, Social Studies, and Sociology. His book publications include: *The Shadow of the Bear*, *Christ at the Dinner Table*, and *Christ in All His Glory*.

B. David Spicer lives in Ohio, where he earned a B. A. in English from Ohio University. He has always been an avid reader and one day woke up and started writing fiction of his own. Along with crime fiction, science fiction and horror fiction he'll occasionally jot down a prose poem or two, though he'll probably deny that in court. He sometimes writes scripts for independent comic book publishers, but short stories are his favorite subjects. He likes board and role-playing games and attending gaming conventions.

Artists' Biographies

Eilee Fahnestock, who designed the cover art and most interior sketches, is a young artist who lives in Idaho with her family, two dogs, five cats, rabbits, chickens, and her horse. She draws inspiration from the beauty she sees in all of creation and hopes to pursue a career in art. She may be contacted at eilee.fahnestock@yahoo.com.

Jeanette Deatherage is the daughter of C. K. Deatherage and contributed the sketch of the kitten at the beginning of the Creature Comforts section. Jeanette loves drawing, dancing, gymnastics, and watching gaming and cooking videos.

CPSIA information can be obtained
at www.ICGtesting.com
Printed in the USA
FFOW04n1539010714
6151FF